The Lives of Pearl

Linda Diane Sickles

The Lives of Pearl
© 2018 Logo en la Cabeza
All rights reserved. This book or any portion thereof may not be reproduced or used in any manner whatsoever without the express written permission of the publisher except for the use of brief quotations in a book review or scholarly journal.
First Printing: 2018
ISBN 978-1-5323-6464-8
Logo en la Cabeza
1310 14th Avenue SW
Olympia, Washington 98502
(360) 359-6650

Acknowledgements

I have many people to thank for the information and support that allowed me to actually complete this project. My sisters including Frances, Susan and Jeannette contributed to the gathering of factual information. Frances researched the Métis part of the family and Susan and Jeannette shared letters and cards they had received over the years from Pearl. In addition, my cousin, Kristi, shared many ancestor photos. I can also thank Kristi for generously sharing the work she had previously done on Ancestry.com. The family stories gleaned from another cousin, Diane, helped me fill in gaps about Pearl and Bart and the children. My friend, Marlene, generously lent me books about prairie life. My sincere thanks go to family and friends who assisted in the editing process. Finally, thanks go to my husband, Robert, for his patient assistance in the revising of this work. In addition, his talents in cover designing and transforming my raw material into a book form were invaluable.

Introduction

As I look back on my life and reflect on my childhood I feel a remarkable gratitude for my parents and grandparents and for the melodies of their enduring love. The "pain" of growing up was only a background beat as the lyrics of joy and connection swept me along.

Now 70, and retired from teaching, I sense there is a story that must be told. This story is not only mine but the sum total of generations of individuals who traveled thousands of miles on ships, wagons, horses, and on foot through prairies, mountains and on rivers, many ending up in the northwest portion of the United States.

I ask myself, "Who are these ghosts lingering in my consciousness begging for expression? Why am I so compelled to make this journey?" My consistent answer harkens back to faith—faith that I am being led to share a wondrous tale filled with hardship, joy, pain, contentment, pride and humility. Each of these attributes we meet upon our pathway to spiritual growth.

Raised in a white, middle class, conservative household, seldom did I think about the roots of my family. The answers to my questions about my heritage—generally spurred by a social studies assignment in school, were short and undefined. "Oh, I think Grandma has French and German in her family." Satisfied at that point, I asked little more and rarely questioned my mother's dark looks, deep set brown eyes or maiden name- Ouellette. On those occasions when a question would come up, my mother's brief, noncommittal answers abruptly ended the discussion.

My father, a blue-eyed redhead with an Irish temper to match was forthcoming to the extent that his generation allowed. His nose to the grindstone attitude and intention to make a better living for his family than the previous one, kept him aloof and focused elsewhere. Interested in what happened beyond his grandparents' lifetimes was not high on his list of priorities until his last few years of life. At that point we made a wonderful connection as he shared memories of his childhood and years as a young man before he met my mother. A few tidbits also came up about his great grandfather's life as well.

There was a moment of discovery for me as a young adult when in passing, almost as if this was coming from common knowledge, my mother revealed her Native American heritage. By this time my mother and father had divorced and apparently no longer did my mother feel she had to keep this secret from my father or her daughters. (Although I suspect Dad knew on some level). In addition, the consciousness of shame for admitting to an Indian heritage was beginning to be altered by the open-mindedness of a new generation of Americans and it was now becoming common for folks to investigate their "roots."

The baby boomer, liberal, compassionate individual that I was delighted in this news. "My mother is at least 1/4 Indian blood. That makes me 1/8!" was my self-centered revelation. "How special for me!" The news might have ended there, had it not been for my half-sister who took a special interest in genealogy and shared her findings with the family. As she discovered our grandfather's Métis background and produced a family tree going back to the late 1700's, I knew at some point I would want more of this colorful history.

Unfortunately, the serious searching did not come about until after Grandma had passed on and we discovered family members who came from European, German, and Swiss roots living in Minnesota. Circumstances led Grandma to marry into a culture having Indian and French blood whose people had worked as traders, farmers, buffalo hunters, and trappers in both Canada and the United States.

My experience, after gathering oral histories, genealogical records and research publications, has left me yearning for more contact with my ancestors. That these individuals led lives nearly unheard of in current times goes without saying. Yet there are most assuredly emotional and spiritual connections as we feel our own turmoil, yearn for love, and strive for success. These are exactly the same human experiences no matter the decade, no matter the family. As the tale began to unwind before me, I joined my great grandparents in Minnesota, traveled with my grandma to

North Dakota, and then on into the depths of this Métis culture of which I am a part. My Métis grandfather was only a part of my family's life for a short time. But the birth of my mother, the Ouellette name, and perhaps the intricate bonds and kinship ties for which the Métis have come to be known, have called to me to join them in spiritual communion.

This book should be considered historical fiction. Much is assumed or written from family stories, some is completely made up for lack of adequate factual material, and some is based upon documents and historical facts. All of it is written from the heart of an individual who hopes to connect with the spirits of those no longer in human form but whose presence can be felt as guiding rays of light. I will introduce you first to my great grandmother, Mary Schultz.

Chapter 1

As the pretty, bright eyed young woman walked with confidence through the plank door on this spring morning in 1891, the tinkle of a bell seemed to announce her arrival. With a knowing smile, she crossed the threshold to what she was certain would be the next important step along her life's journey. Mary expected only good, and she was delighted by what she saw in the newly opened mercantile shop: bright and beautiful bolts of cloth, matching thread, and gorgeous yarns. Her friend had been right about this lovely shop, but instinctively Mary knew that it held much more for her than merchandise. As Mary expressed her desire to find work, the clerk took in her charming face, confidence, and poise, and suddenly remembered a family in the community she had heard needed some domestic help.

"Ah, this will be my adventure," thought Mary.

Never really believing in coincidence, but in a higher power somehow directing her, Mary thought back to all the times in her life when her intuition had been her guiding force. Mary's aunt had called it her niece's "active imagination," but Mary knew differently. Mary would so clearly be aware that something of importance was about to happen. Always close to her siblings, Mary knew when one of them was in trouble. There were also times when a vision would suddenly appear and Mary would steel herself for a knock on the door announcing an accident or illness connected with someone she knew. Her gift would often lead her to happy surprises, like the morning she knew a special, furry kitten would turn up in the barn. This faith in an all knowing all loving source had allowed Mary to deal, even at a young age, with the death of her father.

Mary Schultz had been a child born from the love between two German immigrants who had come to America with the hope of providing a secure and prosperous life for their family. Life in Germany was difficult, and the prospect of a better one in America was their dream. Overcrowded conditions, the unavailability of jobs, and the high taxes had led the family to immigrate to New York in 1873. Mary had not been born yet, but her father and mother had her sisters Minny, Zelma, Elisa, and baby Emma. Mary's mother, Sophia, described the trip and the landing in New York as one of confusion and worry. Prayers were a constant source of faith that all would be well. The family found housing in a crowded tenement near other German immigrants and Mary's father, Lewis, found work. It was here that Mary's brave mother and father managed their first two years in a challenging new country.

During the family's stay in the city, Lewis had met other families who were saving their hard-earned dollars to travel west so they might obtain land of their own. Some of them had taken the opportunity to homestead in Minnesota which was described as a beautiful, wild country with acres of land available in which a family could realize its dreams—a place where children could be raised with clean air, abundant food, and where there would be numerous possibilities for employment in this up and coming part of the country. Mary's family happily settled in Spring Hill, Minnesota in 1875.

Life was good in this new community. The Schultz's worked hard building their simple home, and were very pleased with the offers of help from others who had made the journey west earlier than they. With the acquired acreage, Lewis began to farm the rich land and raise dairy cattle. Sophia, Mary's mother, worked right alongside her husband, happy to be in a land with open spaces and the promised fresh air.

Sadly, about 10 years after their arrival in this new country, tragedy struck the family. Mary was 10 years of age when her father died. By this time, she had 12 siblings. Her mother, Sophia, was distraught and overwhelmed by the prospect of raising the children alone. Mary often held her mother's hand and spoke soothingly to her that all would be well. She assured Sophia that her father's spirit would be guiding the family. Fortunately, Lewis left the family with land and money on which to live. After a time, a suitor began to visit Sophia and she gradually became a joyful person again.

By the time Mary reached 16 years of age, she felt a need to strike out on her own and see what experiences might come her way. The young girl set her sights on Cold Spring, a town about 25 miles from Spring Hill where a friend of Mary's had moved recently. Allowing providence to guide her, and with words of encouragement from her family, she began her search for a position. New possibilities put a smile on Mary's face. With the address of a prospective employer tucked in her bag, Mary set out. Her eyes were shining, and her open mind made her look as if she had a special secret and she would be more than happy to share it.

Arriving at the house, Mary commanded her butterfly-filled stomach to calm, walked around to the back as she had learned was the custom for hired help, and rang the bell. Mary was ushered in by the cook, a jolly sort, who explained that Mrs. Weins would soon join Mary. One imagines that when Mrs. Weins first met Mary her look would have mesmerized the lady of the house. How could anyone not be completely charmed?

Mary gratefully accepted the position in a lovely home that she understood housed Mr. and Mrs. Weins, their daughter, Margaretha, and three grandchildren. Not unlike the tasks she had done at home, Mary began spending her days doing seemingly endless duties: cleaning up after others, washing, folding, changing, and scrubbing. Still, Mary considered herself to be blessed to have found a job so quickly. Besides, these activities were such a small part of Mary's existence.

Mary considered her life so much more than what she did. What Mary was BEING was the essence of Mary. This young girl's outer life would reflect the inner life of a romantic soul who would, for example, look out her small attic window and feel the sun's warmth, be charmed by the filtering light dancing on her small end table, or be taken away with the song of the early morning robin announcing his pleasure with life. Mary was grateful for every day and rarely allowed her busyness to keep her from finding joy in her day. Always, the underlying truth of Mary's life was to be present in whatever task she was doing and to feel gratitude for being able to do it. Awareness of each sensation, be it the softness of the sheets, the swishing of the broom, or the fragrance of the cook's latest creation, all of it meant Mary was alive and able to look forward to whatever the next experience might be. All the better if the adventure involved another person with whom Mary could connect—that would make her feel more alive than anything.

One especially sunny, bright day Mary had a feeling of excitement and impending change. As she descended the back staircase on her way to the kitchen, a tall, impossibly handsome young man bolted out the kitchen door with a smile on his face and clutching a fist full of chocolate cookies. These favorite treats had been given him by the cook whose pleasure it was to spoil Henry, the charming eldest grandchild of the house. At that moment, Henry's face expressed amazement as he nearly collided with the lovely vision before him. Barely registering the crisp, white apron over the simple cotton shift or the scarf tied loosely over her hair where dark curls were escaping, Henry's eyes locked onto the most beautiful, glowing blue eyes he had ever seen. When Henry and Mary gazed at each other, the small alcove was alight with the spirits of these two young people. An illusion perhaps, but there was an electricity in the air that spoke of something special. Mary clearly believed that the eyes are the mirrors of the soul. In that moment of recognition, she experienced a clear vision of Henry becoming an important part of her life.

Henry very properly reached out to shake the hand of this lovely young girl as he croaked, "Hello, I'm Henry Mattman." Not capable of more than that, Henry's smiling face and bright eyes told the story of his feelings.

Mary, with a similar sparkle in her eyes responded, "Hello, I'm Mary Schultz and so very glad to meet you."

Henry was immediately taken with this sprite of a girl who looked him right in the eyes, not wavering for a second. In fact, he had the distinct impression that he knew her from some time long ago, another life perhaps. The moment he entertained such a notion, he wondered if he had taken leave of all his senses or become mesmerized by the vision before him and he laughed out loud at himself! Henry became aware of how impressed he was with the fact that Mary did not look shyly away even though he knew that some members of the community might deem that bold action unseemly for a housemaid. To the contrary, Henry appreciated the value of everyone he met and was sensitive to Mary's self-assuredness. In fact, everything about Mary spoke of confidence and poise and something else Henry couldn't quite put his finger on but which he intended to discover as soon as possible.

After their chance encounter Mary asked the cook just who this young man was. She had met Anna, age 15, and Leo, age 14, and was told there was a third grandchild who Mary assumed must be this handsome young man named Henry.

At first, Henry was very careful to approach Mary only when no one could intrude on their meeting. Henry feared his grandfather's reaction concerning the impropriety of initiating a friendship with the hired help. He realized that as a result of his grandfather's business success, there was a certain snobbishness in his opinions of others he considered less successful than he. Certainly Henry, who had come to live with grandfather at the age of 7 when his father died, had not been raised to discriminate or place himself above others and he did not approve of this condescending attitude. And so began a plan of action in Henry's mind to acquaint himself with this startlingly lovely creature.

One day, Henry lingered in the hallway at the back of the house hoping to "accidentally" bump into Mary. Imagine his surprise when he felt a presence behind him. As he turned, he discovered the object of his interest standing before him.

It's now or never," thought Henry nervously. "Mary, I was wondering if, when you are off duty, you might like to accompany me on a little walk to the park."

If Mary noticed Henry's nervousness, she did not let on and softly whispered her assent to his request. Henry again marveled at his strong attraction to this young girl. Having had very little experience with the company of the opposite sex other than his mother, grandmother, or sister, this was a new and remarkable, if not perplexing, feeling for him. To most people Mary would be considered a pleasant looking young girl but certainly no beauty. Nevertheless, there was something there that drew them to each other.

The two young people chose a bluff overlooking a lake, sat on a blanket Henry had thoughtfully brought along, and began to become acquainted. Henry explained a little about his grandfather who had emigrated from Luxembourg, Belgium, where he had met and married his wife Maria. The couple had ended up in Illinois where they had two children and eventually moved to Minnesota where Grandfather had begun homesteading. Two more children were born. Henry explained that his grandfather had worked hard at farming, and had expected his children to take over the farm one day. Each of the children, however, had found other avenues of interest and had moved on. Henry's grandfather had been a wise businessman and had made investments, particularly in the railroad, and was ready now to take it easy.

As Mary learned a little about Henry's family, she began to sense a connection between the two. The warmth she felt when looking in Henry's eyes was as real as Mary had ever experienced, and yet she suspected there was much more to this young man. Mary was increasingly anxious to get to know all she could about Henry.

Before long, Mary and Henry would capture time to meet in the garden or stroll along the lake on Mary's day off. Henry should have been worried lest he meet one of his grandfather's associates but amazingly, when he was in the presence of his new friend, Henry's worries disappeared. Because he felt so comfortable with Mary, he began to share his hopes and dreams. The two were developing a trust in each other.

"Mary, I was young when my father left us, but not so young that my memories are not true and distinct. I hold both the joyous ones which resulted from my too brief years knowing such a loving father and the painful ones when I recall my mother's grief as she explained to me that Father had gone forever to live among the angels. That thought I could never grasp, but I held tightly to the love Father and I shared."

Mary's response gave Henry all the more impetus to continue disclosing his feelings as he realized just how much the two had in common. For Mary's part, as she saw Henry's vulnerability and his willingness to connect with her, the words spilled from within and she felt no shyness at all.

"Henry, my dear parent was taken from me at a young age too. Like you, the love I shared with my father continues to be the strong bond between us. Often his presence is with me, and I know his spirit will never die just as the spirit of your father will remain a guiding light to you forever."

Never having thought about his father in terms of spirit or light, Henry felt his mind opening to these new insights introduced by this amazing new friend. He continued to share his thoughts.

"You know, Mary, Grandfather Weins expects me to go off to college next year, take animal husbandry, and come back to take over the farm. In my heart of hearts it isn't at all what I want to do." Henry began to tell that which he had told no one before: how much he yearned to follow in his other grandfather, Peter Mattman's footsteps. Henry's grandfather had made the journey from Switzerland to land as an immigrant in New York and had lived with Henry's mother and father. As a young child Henry remembered watching his Grandfather Mattman using his hands to make the most wonderful wooden toys and furniture. He also took the lead in building the home that Henry lived in until he came to live with Grandfather Weins.

Henry's eyes lit up as he explained, "Mary, I watched my Grandfather Mattman and my father work together whenever Father had time from his farming duties. I remember as such a young child knowing I would someday become a craftsman like he was. We were so lucky to have Grandfather as long as we did and we were very sad when he passed away. As often as possible, even though I was very young, Father would allow me to work with tools and scraps of wood to make my treasures."

But when tragedy struck the family, with the loss of Henry's father, his mother, sister, and younger brother, out of necessity, went to live with Grandfather Weins. "Losing Father and being uprooted from my home was difficult, but on some level I understood that Mother had no choice," related Henry with a faraway look as his thoughts called forth the past.

Consequently, Henry was always very respectful and grateful to his grandfather and knew that he had taken them in when there were no other alternatives. But the two households were as different as night and day. Henry and his father had laughed and sung and just plain enjoyed life. Grandfather, on the other hand, was all serious, stern and very, very proper.

As Mary listened with keen interest, Henry spoke of the times he had spent with his father and grandfather, fascinated to watch these men turning the legs of a dining room table on a wood lathe or carving an intricate design on a headboard. The two had lovingly and painstakingly taught Henry all they knew of the ways to bring life to the beautiful pieces being created. Even at a very young age, Henry could spend hours watching his father's craft.

"I was in awe watching hands transform wood into a piece filled with life," explained Henry reverently. "I was allowed to help as much as my young body was able. I enjoyed those times when I certainly learned some skills, but more importantly, I loved being next to Father and Grandfather's strong countenances as they gently taught me to respect the wood and my part in allowing it to become a treasure."

Henry again related just how devastated he felt for a time after the death of both of these men. He realized that his father had become someone who seemed to really see Henry as a person not just a little child, and he began to look up to him and want to be just like his hard-working father.

Henry explained, "As I began to accept the death of this great man, I vowed to do something with my life that would honor my father and serve myself as well. My fondest wish is to do as my father and Grandpa Mattman did and use my gifts to create for others. When I first moved here with Grandfather Weins, I tried to explain to him what I wanted to do with my spare time but Grandfather had other ideas. Certainly, I knew

I had to help with the farm chores but I felt Grandfather scorned me for my wish to work with wood."

Mary noticed how the light in Henry's eyes glowed as he spoke about this ambition. "I know that my grandfather considers this a childish pipe dream and no way for the offspring of a Weins to make a living." Just as quickly, Mary watched Henry's passion burn out. The thought of his grandfather's expectations brought sadness to Henry's eyes.

It had been made clear that foregoing this opportunity in favor of working with wood would be the height of foolishness and not permissible. Grandfather imagined that sending Henry off to college would result in maturity and a newfound realization that financial security is the most important goal in life. Henry's mother, Margaretha, had a much softer view of things, remembering how much her husband loved both Henry and his art. However, she was very afraid of the wrath of this man who supported her children.

Taking Henry's face in her hands and gazing clearly into his eyes, Mary spoke from her heart. "It must be painful to be at such odds with your grandfather. But I see how passionately you speak of your aspirations. Never take your dreams lightly. I have always believed that we are led to make the choices which bring us happiness and fulfillment. Only you can make these choices. Continue to look within and your answers will come." Mary lovingly shared her thoughts with this man who was becoming so important to her.

Henry loved his grandfather so this situation lay heavily upon him. He was convinced that the secret in Mary's eyes, the look that had so entranced him, had to do with knowing the truth about what is really important in life. At this moment Henry saw in Mary a comrade, someone who understood the love he felt for his grandfather and yet the vision he had for himself. Not since his father's death had he felt so attuned to another.

As Henry learned of Mary's life and felt her persistent joy, he fell in love with this amazing young woman and began to make plans to include her in his future. On a beautiful sun dappled afternoon, when the couple was sitting in the sun on a park bench overlooking the town square, Henry approached Mary with the most important question he had ever asked. "Mary, there is something I must say." With twinkling eyes, Henry confessed that he had fallen in love with Mary's gentleness of spirit and joy in life. "You would make me the happiest man in the world if you would be my wife."

Mary, delighted and not entirely surprised by this question, did pause for a moment's reflection. Indeed, Mary loved Henry deeply, but she wondered for Henry's sake just what a union such as theirs would mean. She was, of course, just the maid and she had come to learn a bit about her employer's prejudices. Despite Mary's practical side, she could no more have said no to Henry's proposal than she could have stopped her loving heart.

"Henry, I have known since the day you bounded from the kitchen and we nearly collided that you would mean a great deal to me. Little did I know just how much. Of course, I will marry you."

On top of the world at that moment, Henry and Mary were about to learn firsthand that their capacity for love would face difficult trials. Henry's plan was to take Mary with him to Grandfather's office where he knew the elder would be this time of the morning, but Mary cautioned Henry that he might wish to speak to his grandfather privately about the couple's plans and have her join him afterwards.

So, filled with the elation of young love, Henry knocked on the library door and heard a gruff, "Come in." He approached his grandfather's imposing figure. "Grandfather I would very much like to discuss with you a matter of utmost importance."

Reluctantly, Henrich raised his eyes from the book which apparently held such interest to him at the moment and blurted, "Well, get on with it!"

Despite his fears, Henry began to tell Henrich of his feelings and intentions for Mary. Henry had always known his grandfather to be old fashioned and concerned with constraints that the Weins' place in the community might have on such a union. Deep down, though, Henry couldn't really imagine a scenario in which he wouldn't eventually understand the deep love Henry held for Mary and want only the best for him. But on this day when he announced his devotion to Mary Schwartz, Henry felt the bitter taste of cruelty.

"You cannot be serious!" shouted Henrich. "Have you taken leave of your senses? No such liaison shall take place. I should have known no good would come from hiring a wench like that girl. She will be fired at once and that will be the end of it!" exploded this red-faced man standing before a stunned and mute Henry.

The arrogance and narrow mindedness with which his grandfather responded overwhelmed him. Henry had never felt himself better than another, no matter the difference in wealth or status. Not so his grandfather. These cruel words hung in the air. The ultimatum was declared. Henrich Weins demanded that Henry find Mary and bring her to him immediately. Standing outside the office door but unable to hear the conversation, Mary heard the door opening and saw the devastated look in Henry's eyes. Henry's shaky hand reached for Mary's and he reluctantly pulled her into the room. When Mary saw the cold, penetrating glare from her employer, she felt tremendous fear for Henry and herself.

"Mary, your services are no longer needed. Pack your belongings and be out of this house by noon," declared the strident voice of Henrich Weins.

"As you wish," replied Mary, now aware that the conversation Henry had had with his grandfather would likely change her life forever. Unsure of just what direction her future would take, Mary wondered if Henry would back down and be unable to marry her. At that instant, she decided that whatever the outcome, life would continue to bless her as long as she did not allow fear to take over. Firm in those convictions, Mary searched Henry's face as the pair took their leave from the library.

Henry swept Mary up to her tiny loft room and sat beside her on the carefully made cot. Gently holding both Mary's small hands in his and looking directly into those beautiful blue eyes, Henry expressed the sorrow he felt at his grandfather's reaction. To Mary he declared, "For you to be treated so shabbily hurts me to my core and I would understand if you were now unable to become the wife of a man whose family is so unfeeling. We will be given nothing from my grandfather. He has made it very clear this marriage will not have his blessing and that, were I to insist on marrying you, he would no longer have a grandson."

Mary was unable to express in words the profound relief that Henry still wanted to marry her because, at the same time, she was also experiencing the pain that emanated from her love's body. She was aware that Henry would be sacrificing so much for her. Nevertheless, Mary pulled him to her and let her heart tell him her answer. Of course she would marry this brave man whom she now realized loved her unconditionally. "I cannot imagine sharing my life with any other," declared Mary.

Certain that their strong proclamations and the firing of this presumptuous maid would be the end of Henry's foolish infatuation, Henrich had seriously underestimated the depth of love his grandson felt for Mary. He would be shocked, and Margaretha devastated, by the events that followed. Henry's determination to fashion a life for himself and his darling Mary, outweighed all other considerations. Knowing that his plans would perhaps estrange him forever from his grandfather, Henry proceeded to plan a future for himself and his wife to be.

Henry had inherited a small nest egg from his beloved father. Tearfully wishing that his father could be with him at that moment, Henry confided in Mary, "I know Father would want us to use this money to begin our lives together. I will start my wood business and make you and Father proud." Mary assured Henry that she could not be more proud, and that surely his father's spirit would be with him every step of the way.

Because Henry had been raised to respect his parents and grandparents, he felt compelled to try once more to reason with Grandfather. Knowing Henrich's habits included a ride on his horse each morning, and with faint hope that this stubborn man would listen to reason, Henry trudged to the barn. Not even the normally joyful song of the bluebird, the gentle sway of the willow tree, or the warm sun rising over the crest of the hill gave Henry much hope. Henry was so familiar with Grandfather's iron will. Though in the past, any confrontations Henry might have had were of minor importance compared to this decision. But being an optimistic young man in love, Henry put a smile on his face and decided to face the dragon. As Henry stepped into the barn, he looked over to see his grandfather staring at him. In the moment when the two men met each other's eyes, a spark of violence was apparent in Grandfather's glare.

"Please Grandfather, may I speak?" asked Henry.

A brief question crossed Grandfather's face followed by, "Have you finally come to your senses?"

Standing tall with shoulders back and determination pouring from him, Henry repeated his decision to marry. "I love her Grandfather."

"You are a fool. Get out of my barn!" shouted Grandfather.

Henry became aware of just how out of control his grandfather had become when he saw the horsewhip in the older man's hand.

"Have you forgotten how much you loved Grandmother when you first met?" declared Henry as he began to back slowly out of the barn.

"How dare you speak of your common hussy in the same breath as my wife? I repeat, you are no longer my grandson if you go through with this!" With that this person who no longer resembled anyone Henry had ever known struck out as if his life depended upon it. A trembling hand and the rage that gave it force snapped the whip at Henry. A scream came out of Henry's mouth as he felt the sting of a thousand needles in his eye and felt blood begin to course down his face.

The next few days were filled with fear, apprehension, and pain both physical and mental. Henry's mother, Margaretha, tended to her son and was deeply sorrowful when the doctor pronounced that Henry had lost his eye as a result of his grandfather's rage. Mary, for her part, had no recourse but to flee to her mother's home and await news. Mary wished to be at her love's side throughout his hospital stay, but Margaretha, terribly afraid of more reprisals from her father, suggested it best that Mary stay away while Henry recovered. Henry convinced his mother that he and Mary were not giving up their relationship and so Margaretha kept Mary current on Henry's condition. In addition, while Henry recuperated at the hospital and at his request, Margaretha packed up Henry's belongings.

Finally, Mary was reunited with her husband to be. With his grandfather's condemning words and outrageous actions echoing in his mind, Henry left the grand house on the hill and traveled across town to meet his love. The moment Henry came into view, Mary could sense the extent of emotional pain pouring from her love's very being, and she begged Henry to share his innermost feelings with her.

Henry felt confident that Mary would not judge him and so expressed his pain. "I am feeling such rage at my grandfather for his treatment of you and his disregard for his own flesh and blood. He is a shallow, prideful, ignorant man. Mother tells me she is certain that he is ashamed of his loss of control but is much too stubborn to back down. How can he not understand how very much in love we are?" The sadness in Henry's face expressed the deep grief he felt at this moment.

Mary responded carefully to her husband to be. "My dear love, the only way I know to heal your broken heart is for you to accept that your grandfather is doing the best he is able at this time."

With a shaky voice, Henry replied, "How can this be his best? Is there no compassion in this man? Mary, I'm not at all sure I can forgive him for turning against you and maiming me. Isn't this more than we should bear?"

Mary explained that Henry's anger and feeling of being out of control was based on fear. Gently Mary said, "My sense is that your grandfather is especially unable to deal with these emotions and so must continue his tirade even at the expense of his relationship with you. Since we in turn have no real control over his mind right now, let us see him with forgiveness. You know your grandfather loves you and always will, and we can only hope this love will someday override what he is feeling."

Henry was not at all certain he could succeed in letting go of his own anger and disappointment enough to see only love, but Henry valued Mary's words and had learned so much from her about life in the short time they had known each other, he promised that he would try to do just that. As the two shared their lives together, this new way of "seeing" began to have an impact on him. Subsequently, upon feeling gloomy or worried over his belief that his grandfather had rejected him, Henry imagined himself embracing Grandfather. Henry felt much better, and he hoped that someday there would be a reunion. Clearly, whether or not Grandfather changed his mind, with Mary's help Henry could see that he needed to change his own.

The couple was married by a justice of the peace in Kandiyohi County on November 11, 1892, and spent their first night in a small inn. Mary's mother's wedding dress fit her perfectly and so the couple commemorated the event with a photo of the two dressed in their finery. They traveled north to Duluth by rail where one of Henry's sisters lived. With her help, they found a small house that was to become a home for the newlyweds. It was here they began their lives in earnest. Mary was delighted to see the charming little house, and as she often did, imagined her father coming to visit, pleased with the handsome young man she had chosen. "But enough of that," thought Mary. "It's high time to make some plans."

Since it was winter their much needed garden would have to wait. Mary began to "pretty up" their space with bright red gingham curtains, homemade candles, and the loving touches that made their house a home. With the tools Henry's father had given him, this excited young man began working with wood. As neighbors began realizing Henry's talent, the orders came in and the business began to flourish. Fond memories of his father accompanied each piece, and Henry grew convinced that Mary was right—"Father's presence is here with me."

On a cold January morning, Mary had a vision of a sweet, cherub face looking up at her from a cradle. "Aha, thought Mary. Just as I dreamed! My prayers have been answered and a little one is on the way." Not sure how to impart the news to her husband, Mary reached out her arms to the face that had grown so precious to her. Henry knew something was up. The starry eyes of his mate were literally dancing with sparkles.

"What's going on, my Mary? You look like the cat that swallowed the canary!"

Mary's reply filled Henry with joy. "We are going to have a baby, dear heart," sang Mary. Henry couldn't have been happier as he grabbed Mary and they danced around their cozy little home. With thoughts of his father, Henry could hardly wait to design a beautiful crib for this welcome child. While creating this gift, Henry began to pray that a child would at last bring his grandfather back into their lives.

Spring came and Mary and Henry began to plant a garden that would sustain them through the long Minnesota winter. Mary had helped her mother in their garden and with the assistance of loving neighbors, the couple began the hard work of their lives. Happily planting the seeds that would nourish them, Mary shared her delight with Henry.

"I feel the grace of God working in our lives." Henry agreed and confided that he had never felt happier.

Unbelievably, the prospect of becoming parents brought even more love into their little home. Henry and Mary's "Pearl" was born early the next fall on the 18th of September, 1893. On that beautiful fall day, Mary was certain her father was there with her, sharing in this most glorious time. In fact, Mary began to feel closer and closer to his spirit as time went by. In the still, quiet night as Mary rocked her baby girl she felt his presence and even began to hum long forgotten tunes of her childhood. Never questioning this revelation, but feeling so blessed to experience such closeness, Mary cherished every moment with Pearl and with these "memories" of her loved one.

For the first few months of Pearl's life, Henry and Mary were bound together in the joy of life, despite the fact that Grandfather Weins had made no effort to see the couple or their precious daughter. Margaretha, however, had been delighted with the tiny bundle and made the trip by train to visit. Henry and Mary both felt that life had blessed them and the pride they felt in their child grew with each new "trick" baby Pearl learned from that first smile at just a few weeks to the first time she rolled over. Now they were three and life grew more and more fulfilling.

But the story takes a tragic turn and Pearl is not to have this wonderful Mother for long. At first, Henry was sure that Mary could fight the illness that had struck his household. He did everything he could to nurse Mary and to take care of little Pearl. In fact, when Mary asked to be taken back home to Spring Hill to be with her mother and family, Henry was happy to oblige. But one night Mary had a very clear vision of her impending passing. Knowing that she had to pave the way as best she could for Henry, she prayed for the right words to lessen Henry's pain.

The next morning, Mary began with these words, "Henry you have been the guiding light in my life this last year. No one could have made me happier nor shown me how cherished I am. You are a strong and capable man, stronger than even you know. I am asking you to draw on that strength now."

"Mary what are you talking about?" Even as he asked the question, he knew. As he looked at his Mary the realization that she was going to leave him and baby Pearl was almost more than he could bear. As the tears rolled down his cheeks, Henry promised Mary that he would be there for Pearl and continue building a life for the two of them.

As Mary's body became weaker from the illness, Henry knew that he had to face the fact that he would be left to raise their daughter alone. More and more Mary had conversations with her father just as if he were preparing the way for her to join him. Trusting that this was exactly what Mary needed, Henry felt that if he was to lose the love of his life, he was content to believe that she would not be alone. Surely she would be among the angels that her mother had spoken of when Henry was a boy.

And so sadly, when Pearl was but eight months old, the shimmering light left Mary's eyes and Henry was left to grieve for the sweet soul who had meant the world to him. Mary's body was laid to rest in a grave at the Paynesville Community Cemetery where her father had been buried. Henry stood at the cemetery with little Pearl in his arms, his tears dropping upon her pink blanket.

Despite his intentions to the contrary, Henry became nearly despondent at his loss. Not only had he lost this precious one, but now he needed to be both mother and father to Pearl. In addition, bills that had been incurred during Mary's illness needed to be paid and Henry had no alternative but to find a way to earn more money. There were monumental decisions to be made. After the service, Henry and baby Pearl boarded the train back to Duluth where he hoped there would be those willing to help him in this time of need. The train trip was difficult. It was as if little Pearl understood the devastating event and Henry was unable to comfort her. Were it not for some caring women on the train, Henry would have been beside himself.

Much to Henry's dismay, relatives were either unwilling or unable to help. Margaretha's hands were tied by grandfather's control and Mary's family had been nearly devastated by the stock market crash that year. Finally, Henry's sister, Anna, who had recently married, agreed to keep Pearl while Henry, out of necessity, took a job in the forest. Unfortunately, Anna's husband was very unhappy with this arrangement and Pearl was passed along to neighbors whom she felt were trustworthy. It was explained to them that Henry would be back to reclaim his daughter when he could afford to. The Brys' had lost two children of their own and so were only too aware of the grief Henry was experiencing.

The love and joining and faith that this couple shared with one another, became, for Henry, sadness and disillusionment and despair. Pearl, the baby who was so treasured, was abandoned by both Mother and Father. The loving neighbors could apparently not face giving Pearl back to her father. Hoping to replace their own lost children in their hearts, the Brys family began referring to Pearl as Leona, and fled their home in Duluth when Henry's child was two years old. Upon return from the forest, Henry was devastated yet again to learn of this deception, an empty house, and address unknown.

Filled with anger and fear and with the limited resources at his disposal, Henry investigated his daughter's disappearance. He questioned his sister, neighbors, friends, shopkeepers, anyone he could think of who might have been aware of the Brys' abrupt move and their whereabouts. He put ads in newspapers and magazines and prayed every day that someone somewhere would know something of his beloved baby. Henry dreamed of the day he would again be able to hold and cuddle Pearl, hear her sweet voice, kiss her soft cheek. He vowed he would never, under any circumstances, leave her alone again.

After many months of searching, Henry knew he had to get back to work not only to support himself but to be distracted from the pain that every moment of his life brought him. Grudgingly, Henry went back to the forest, but not before screaming at the world, at himself for ever leaving Pearl, and at God for forsaking him. Never, however, did Henry regret his marriage to the most loving and caring soul he had ever met, his wife, Mary. Eventually the connection he had shared with Mary and then with Pearl would lead him to continue his life, find new relationships and know that this period of his life was a gift that no one could ever take away from him. He had known the blessing of love.

Afterword

So reader, you have met a portion of my family through my eyes and you have been introduced to the experience of loss. Haven't we all felt such emotion in our lives: abandoned by lovers, by parents, by God. Who of us has not felt this pain? The lives of the individuals on these pages are no different. Struggling with this concept, we fear that the fact that loved ones leave is an expression of our own unworthiness to hold them to us.

Mary, however, teaches us another way to look at life. We see an optimistic, spiritual individual who knows herself to be connected to a larger, infinite presence and therefore to each person she meets as if all part of a divine plan. Although it was necessary for her to deal with grief and loss in her young life, it seemed that Mary's view of abandonment was based on a belief that loved ones never really leave but can be a constant presence in one's heart. Clearly she and her family missed her father when he died, but Mary assured others that loving another meant there is no time when that connection is broken. Loving life as Mary did, she was able to reframe even the tragedies and to surrender to life being life. And what can be a stronger expression of loss than a mother having to leave her small child and her loving husband? Yet, Mary blessed each of them and reminded Henry how up to this task he would be. According to the world, Mary's early death could only be construed as a tragedy. Yet she takes the uplifting role of expressing her gratitude for the time she had to spend with Henry and assuring him of his strength to carry on.

Henry, the shy, artistic, romantic young man was able to allow Mary's loving influence to become a part of his experience. Mary continues to teach us. As Henry shares his grief and anger about the way his grandfather treated him, Mary's advice alludes to looking beyond Grandfather Wein's actions and seeing a man who is calling for love in his own way. It is as if Mary has an inner knowing that Henry's grandfather was doing his best at that moment even though to the world this was a weak and cruel act. Instead, compassion is what is called for. Compassion for a man who had expectations of his grandson taking over the family business and then feeling the fear of facing the worldly concerns and being alone in his old age. Compassion even for the shame and guilt that Grandfather Weins must have felt when his strong reaction resulted in the loss of his grandson's eye. Did he ever come to terms with this? Did he deny the emotions and live the rest of his life with these hidden feelings? Grandfather Weins represents that fearful and angry way of looking at the world that each of us have dealt with in our lives. Seeing each day as a blessing no matter the experience - that is the lesson Mary teaches.

Mary's expressions of love allowed her mate to open to this forgiveness and not allow his emotions to overcome him. Henry was able to temper his anger by opening his heart and trusting that Mary could teach him how to feel compassion for a man whose rage blinded him. The relationship these two young people enjoyed changed both of them. Discovering the deeper truth in every moment, expressing love and forgiveness, these are the gifts we are invited to open, these are the blessings each of us has as we envision our lives and the possibilities within them.

The tragedy of Henry returning from the forest and being unable to find his child is factual. One can only imagine the feelings of loss he must have experienced having lost both his wife and then his daughter. Mary died when Pearl was 8 months old. I have a copy of a letter written by my grandmother explaining that Henry took baby Pearl to Duluth to his sister's but that "they didn't want me, especially the husband of the one who had me. My father had to go to the woods for work and in his absence they gave me away to strangers."

The census records show that Henry's sister, Anna, was married and living in Duluth, as was the Brys family. A census record shows that the Brys' had Pearl when she was 2 and they still lived in Duluth but had changed her name to Leona Brys. An adoption paper was discovered by a family member but there was no signature by Henry Mattman. The family story was that Henry had been looking for Pearl for years. Whether Henry ever forgave the Brys' for moving and leaving no forwarding address will remain a mystery. It is clear that it took over 10 years before Henry remarried and had more children.

As I examine these characters that have appeared before me on the pages of this story, I know each of them to be aspects of myself passed down from my ancestors. This inheritance gives me the opportunity to know myself more fully. Always, from my first conscious thoughts as a little girl, there were moments when I recognized a deep knowingness that within me was a light, an aliveness, a truth. This feeling of peace often accompanied me. Mary's personality clearly contained a high degree of this awareness and, like Mary, I have eventually been able to face my fears and trials and draw loving experiences my way. Mary was a young woman of spiritual wisdom. For the most part in the last few years, I have been able to see all of life as a blessing.

Not unlike Grandfather Weins, there is a shadow part of me that reacts when I feel I've lost control or when I am in that space of needing to be right. In these instances ego can take over and it is so easy to be convinced that another has behaved unacceptably and therefore there is justification for judgment. Teaching a classroom of children, as I did for many years, or raising two daughters were occasionally springboards for that kind of passionate reacting.

I thank you Mary and Henry and Henrich for being a part of the matrix of my life. You, and all the generations before and after, are related to me in the current definition of family but also in the broader sense of mankind. I feel your energy, your love, your grief, your pain---We are ONE on this path of LIFE!

Mary Schwartz Mattman

Henry Mattman, on his wedding day

Baby Pearl

Mary's Grave, Paynesville, Minnesota

Chapter 2

As curiosity got the better of her, Leona peered around the corner of the house to get a look at the man with the deep voice she had heard. Leona suspected it was the farm laborer she had seen from the window of her room and who had been working for about a week with Papa on the harvest. Not a large man but obviously a strong one, Leona had noticed the dark, sultry eyes and heavy brows and the gentle way he moved as he did the chores Papa set out for him.

Leona was surprised at her own interest in this man. Up to this point, she had not fancied any of the young men with whom she came in contact. At nearly 16, she felt out of place with those in her own age group. Always a quick and able student, Leona valued her studies and books above all else. In fact, other people did not seem to be drawn to Leona's aloof and distant nature. Truth to tell, all Leona really cared about was her dream of higher education and becoming an architect. This were rarely far from her mind. For a daughter of farmers living in a small rural community, this was a lofty, and some might say, unreasonable dream indeed.

In fact, by the time Leona was 12 she had grown beyond what was being taught in the small one-room prairie schoolhouse. Luckily, her teacher saw in Leona a quick mind and a strong motivation to learn. As her instructor was able, she provided Leona with work and materials outside of the classroom so her learning could continue. She had obtained as many books on as many subjects as she could, and the young girl devoured them.

Leona's able intelligence began plotting a way she could meet this stranger without drawing attention from her parents, especially her mother. Unfortunately, Leona's experience with her mother had taught her to be wary of Delia's moods. Although it had been a while since her mother had flown into a rage, Leona had built such distrust over the years, she was very careful not to do anything that might upset her unpredictable mother. Perhaps helping in the kitchen and then offering to deliver the food to the barn would work. "Mama would probably faint," thought Leona.

"Mama, would you like some help making the supper today for the hired hands?" asked Leona nervously.

Mama Brys's expression of surprise and her reply told Leona that this was a good day. Leona breathed a sigh of relief as she heard her mother say, "That would be very fine indeed. I was just beginning to make some biscuits to go with the stew I started this morning. Why don't you finish that task while I fill the milk pitcher?"

Leona was grateful that she had caught her mother in a seemingly approachable mood, and that Delia did not suspect her new "helpfulness" as a ploy. Consequently, Leona was free to investigate these unexpected feelings that were completely out of character. Although very puzzled at her own reactions, the next step would normally be to begin speculating and analyzing. Instead, Leona began humming to herself. In fact, Leona suddenly realized that she was enjoying the sensation of the dough as she kneaded it and then carefully rolled it on the counter before cutting and placing the plump, white biscuits on the cooking sheet. All the while Leona's mind was drifting away as if some unseen force had taken over.

Normally, Leona's concentration centered on information of one topic or another that she had borrowed from her teacher. Leona's mother only required that she help at breakfast time, gather the eggs, milk the cow, and work in the garden, Leona's favorite task. Because Leona seemed to enjoy sewing, that was another activity that filled her hours at home. The rest of the time left Leona in her room studying and to Delia's way of thinking, out of Delia's way.

As Delia saw the lightly browned biscuits come out of the oven, she was pleased to see that Leona was becoming a good cook despite the infrequent times she spent in the kitchen. "It is about time Leona took an active role in helping me in the kitchen. At least her sewing skills have improved and she seems to have a green thumb and is willing to spend hours in the garden with her vegetables and flowers," thought Delia.

"Very well done, Leona. Those will do nicely. I'm sure the men will appreciate your efforts." At the same time she said this, Leona was aware that Delia looked at her with a confused expression. In fact, Delia could not fathom the reason for the dreamy, vacant look on the face of this normally practical and serious girl.

Since Leona was so rarely praised by her mother, and their relationship had been one of nearly constant turmoil for as long as Leona could remember, the young girl wondered if her mother was able at long last to accept Leona as a valued person rather than a thorn in her side.

"Would you like to take the supper out to the barn and set it up on the table in there?" Leona's flushed cheeks and her mumbled response added to Mama Brys's curiosity as to this change in the girl. "Perhaps the warmth of the day and the heat of the oven have added to Leona's color," thought Mama. "No matter. This daughter of mine will have to know something about taking care of a home and family and now's as good a time as any."

As Leona carried the basket along the dusty path to the barn, she was only slightly aware of the smell of the newly mown hay or the sound of the clomping and snorts of the work horse as some of the men came in from the field. Instead she was worrying about what she might say to a particular laborer if she were given an opportunity. The basket was heavy, and as she approached the barn, heart pounding and hands perspiring, Leona observed her father and this mystery man washing up at the well near the barn. It was difficult for Leona not to stare but she greedily examined the muscular arms and the dark skin and hair on her handsome stranger. Again, Leona was astounded by her own thoughts!

Determined not to let her nervousness be apparent, Leona announced in as strong a voice as she could muster, "Papa, I've brought supper to set up in the barn."

Somewhat startled to see Leona in the service of this task rather than his wife, Lewis, Leona's father, smiled and replied, "How nice to see you out here, Leona." Although Leona was trying not to be obvious, her father noticed the vacant expression on his daughter's face and the shy looks she gave his employee. "Leona, this is John Ouellette."

Close enough now to see the deep set eyes, strong features, and dark hair of this man, Leona wondered if John was of mixed Indian blood. His last name sounded distinctly French. She remembered that Papa had spoken of some men who often came south from Canada and other parts of North Dakota and Montana this time of year to help with the harvest. Leona did recall one occasion, when she was younger, of traveling with her father to a trading post where she observed some who had similar features to Mr. Ouellette. Although Leona had been aware of the term Métis or mixed blood youth who occasionally worked on the farm, she had never been particularly interested in their lives. In fact, although she had not been raised to be judgmental, Leona had heard some disparaging remarks about the Métis from her community. She readily dismissed the comments but now wondered about them. Leona thought harshly of herself for a moment and wished she had taken time to educate herself a little more so she could at least strike up an intelligent conversation. Leona intended to take care of that oversight as soon as she was able. Forcing herself to look directly at John, Leona saw or imagined she saw a sparkle in those deep brown eyes as he gazed directly at her and Leona's tongue was instantly tied.

"Tawnshi!-Hello Leona. I will carry your basket if you do not mind." John's accent was strongly French which Leona recognized from her studies, but there was something else unfamiliar to her in his pattern of speech and, of course, she did not recognize his greeting to her either.

Dazed, Leona followed John into the barn and began unpacking the lunch, carefully placing the items on the table and hoping John would not notice the slight tremor in her hands.

"Whatever is the matter with me?" thought Leona. "I must be losing my mind." Hurriedly before she could make a complete fool of herself, Leona began to retreat saying she would be back to the barn later to pick up the basket. Nearly tripping over her feet, Leona dashed back toward the house, but decided to postpone her return until she felt more in control of herself. She headed for her private place behind the garden where she had placed a stool so she could relish the warmth of the days which would all too soon turn cold in this northern state.

There, sitting amid the bright, yellow sunflowers in Mama's garden, Leona felt thoroughly embarrassed by her infantile behavior and completely confused by the burgeoning feelings that were vying for her attention. Vowing to act like a self-assured person the next time she encountered John, Leona examined her feelings. The truth was that expressing emotion was unfamiliar to this young girl. Always a somewhat somber child, Leona rarely let her guard down as if she experienced a strong need to protect herself from connecting with others. Due to her mother's erratic behavior, she often felt out of place, as if her presence in this simple farming family was a mistake and she actually did not belong here. Chiding herself often, Leona would force herself to join in family activities when her mother's mood would warrant it. Her father was good to her, never harsh or demanding although not especially affectionate. In order to protect herself from more hurt, Leona held herself separate believing herself to be unloved. Often denying this very real feeling, Leona moved through life allowing her intellect to speak for her.

Late the next afternoon, Leona was reading a book underneath the pine tree in the front yard, when Mr. Ouellette walked up to her.

"I have completed my chores. After I wash up would you care to take a walk with me?" John asked in his strange but not unpleasant manner.

"Yes, I believe I would," replied Leona. Leona had done some research and found that John was indeed of mixed Indian and French blood and that her father had known John's father years ago and knew something of his family. Beyond that, Leona was anxious to learn all she could about John and his roots.

"Good, I will be back, Miss Brys."

Hearing her name on his lips gave Leona a thrill. She rushed into the house to comb her hair, pinch her cheeks, and put away her books. Becoming brave in the face of her desire to be with this man, Leona dared to quickly and firmly say, "Mama, I am taking a little walk and will be back later." Not waiting for a response, Leona scurried out the door and saw John waiting by the front gate. There began the first of many such "strolls" and the beginning of an unexpected friendship developing between them.

Delia and Lewis began to notice that John and Leona met by the garden gate each afternoon. Delia had witnessed such starry-eyed expressions on Leona's face lately. Lewis told his wife that Leona had shyly asked him questions about John and his family. The two discussed what it might be like for Leona if she were to become serious about John. Although the Brys' had no such prejudices, they knew that many in the community did not respect the Métis people even though they often hired them on their farms. Lewis felt only positive things toward these hardworking people.

John was very taken with this smart and pretty young woman. He had not met any white woman who was as interested as she in his heritage. For the most part, John was often made to feel inferior within the white community In fact, Leona's questions reminded John of the pride in his family he had always had but rarely allowed himself to think about.

Leona learned that John's full name was Jean Baptiste Ouellette and that his father, Antoine-Arate, had married Angelique Bottineau. They all were a mixture of Chippewa, Cree and French. Leona, always the student, wanted John to share his family's life as far back as he was able. John remembered the many treasured stories he had heard as a child while his large family, including parents, grandparents, brothers, sisters, aunts, uncles and cousins, sat around the campfire on the warm evenings of summer. John explained that his heritage is part French and part Indian and thus was referred to as Métis, a French word meaning mixed. John shared that for many generations, Canada's Native people were enlisted by the French traders to participate in the fur industry. The Native men were skilled in hunting buffalo and the women just as skilled in dressing the skins. The intermarriage of the native women and the French traders brought forth a new culture of people referred to as Métis.

"Our people were raised to appreciate Native and European cultures. My family speaks a combination of languages, the Catholic religion is what is practiced, and we also include many French traditions. We even have a flag which explained the pride in what we do and who we are. I was raised to be proud of my people."

John declared these facts with such force and yet with such sadness, Leona knew that John must be experiencing many underlying emotions of hurt and pain. She chose only to listen carefully and show John how much she cared. John continued his story.

Antoine, John's father, had told of the fun the family had during the evenings after working hard during the day. "Singing old French songs, dancing and being together were fond memories that I loved hearing about and, in fact, remember from my childhood," declared John with a faraway look in his eyes.

"John, one day my father traveled to a trading post at Pembina which is not that far from here and I went with him. We saw the carts loaded with buffalo robes. I remember them because they were so noisy! Is this how your people hauled their robes?" asked Leona.

"Yes, Leona. I think your father met my father at Pembina. They had some business together and that is how their friendship began. Your father was an unusual farmer in that he had no prejudices against our people and attempted to communicate as best he could. Our people always appreciate those who do not see our differences as something to be afraid of."

After one of the serious discussions this new couple engaged in, they took a walk along the path toward the stream. Leona watched John out of the corner of her eye. With butterflies in her stomach and warmth that could not be accounted for by the weather, Leona realized how fond she was growing of John. As if he had heard her thoughts, John reached over and gently took Leona's hand in his. With this handsome man at her side Leona began to dream.

One day John greeted Leona with "Tawnshi" followed by "Miiyoukiishikaw."

"John, what language are you speaking? I would love to learn some of your words."

John explained that the language is a combination of languages and is unique to the Métis. "We call it Michif. I said Hello. It is a nice day."

After the lesson, Leona always greeted John with "Tawnshi and Miiyoukiishikaw" as a way of honoring John's heritage.

This starry-eyed girl was fascinated with everything about John and urged him to continue sharing his family's history. John did just that. Over the course of the harvest season in which he was working for Mr. Brys, the stories of his apparent love of his family and the joyous times they had together made her feel happy for him. At the same time, Leona become aware of what she had missed in her upbringing.

Getting through the day's chores as quickly as possible, each afternoon Leona would comb her hair and anticipate the time she was able to spend with John. One day the sweet hand holding turned into something else and Leona was given her first kiss. The shyness she had felt with John was disappearing and Leona hardly recognized herself. She felt herself passionately responding to John and imagining that she could never be separated from him.

Leona had become dependent upon John's handsome face and dear company. She knew the day would come when John's work with Mr. Brys was completed and he would leave the farm. All too soon Leona was forced to say goodbye to John "Oh John, I will miss you. It can be a dreary life here on the prairie in the winter. Where will you go?"

John's reply made Leona even more interested to hear the rest of the tale about the Métis people. John mentioned that he had been born in Canada but had spent most of his life in Lewistown, Montana. There were still many of his relatives who had settled there and were expecting him before winter set in. Sixteen-year-old Leona felt as if her heart was breaking but she was assured John would be back the next summer.

The couple expressed their goodbyes, kissed and embraced and parted so reluctantly. Seeing tears in Leona's eyes, John promised, "I will be back, Leona. This is not the end of our relationship."

The day John left was a heartbreaking one because Leona had never felt this close to another human being in her life. But within a short period of time after John left, circumstances at the Brys farm changed drastically. Leona had no more time to grieve the loss of John. Delia became very ill. Despite doctor's visits and the nursing with which Leona devoted herself, by winter's end, Delia succumbed to the illness that racked her lungs.

It was a huge task for Leona to take over the chores in the household. Through the family's grief, Leona had to step up to the cooking and cleaning. She and Lewis began to depend upon each other for everything. Fortunately, the community was close knit and there were many wonderful neighbors who came daily to shed some light on these two sad souls. Lewis and Leona would get out on Sundays to attend Mass and see that life did go on. Whenever Leona could spare a small amount of time she would visit her best friend Zada, and share her conflicted feelings about the death of her mother.

Spring came and the work on the farm began anew. There were crops to be planted, animals to be fed and little time for worries or woes. Leona began to wonder if John would be back to help on the farm. She had little time or energy to even broach the subject with her father. Both of them were so weary by day's end, little conversation ensued. But one evening, Lewis told of an influx of Métis help coming into the area the next day. Knowing that Leona would be interested to see John again, he mentioned one Mr. Ouellette was expected.

That night as Leona crawled under her quilt, her often depressed state of mind began to spin with fears and worries that tomorrow would not bring the meeting with John she hoped for. Oh, how she had missed the conversations they had shared. Many more questions about John's family had come up in Leona's mind and she could hardly wait to look into the depth of this man's eyes once more. What was she thinking? What if John does not care anymore? Leona suddenly began to feel shy since so much time had passed. She wondered if the connection she had felt with John would remain. Chiding herself for allowing her mind to take such notions, Leona began a night of much tossing and turning and dreams that awakened her with an emptiness that she could not dispel. Finally, as light shone through Leona's curtains, she rolled out of bed and decided to face the day no matter what it might bring.

Fortunately, the morning brought renewed hope and Leona's heart fluttered with the prospect of seeing John again. She spent the early morning hours assisting the cook whom Father had hired during this time of year in order to feed the hired hands. This would be her first view of John in a year and she wondered if her feelings were still ones of attraction and interest or was this just a young girl's fancy? What if she had imagined the interest in John's eyes? What if their closeness was just a fantasy? Leona's fears again grew as the day wore on.

That afternoon, Leona peeked through the curtains to see if John had remembered their meeting place by the garden gate. Her heart lurched as she spotted John and with little forethought, Leona dashed out the door. Halfway to the garden gate, Leona shyly looked up and into the bright eyes of someone she had so longed to see again. John's face lit up with Leona's presence and the couple reached out to embrace each other.

Leona's natural honesty came to the forefront as she declared, "I could hardly wait to see you today. I have longed to be able to be near you, to touch you and speak of that which is close to my heart."

Blushing mercilessly, Leona lowered her eyes, bit her tongue and wondered what in the world she had been thinking when John said, "How glad I am to hear you speak of such things. I have missed you more than I can say." John's passionate kiss told the story Leona had longed to hear.

As if no time had passed since their last meeting, the couple began to express all they had been unable to say during the months of separation. John asked Leona about her mother and the long winter of caring for her and the feelings she experienced during and afterwards. John proved to be such an intent listener, Leona was moved to share feelings with him that she had expressed to no one, including herself. As Leona explained her childhood to John and the unhappy relationship she had had with her mother, she began to feel some of the heaviness release from her being. She painfully spoke of those times her mother's punishments were extreme. Leona remembered only too well the claustrophobic feelings of being locked in a closet for hours on end. As a young girl, Leona learned to stay out of Delia's way until her father came in from work on the farm and her mother seemed to relax. In the course of speaking from her heart, Leona began to understand how grateful she had been for the change in her mother and the nearly comfortable relationship they were developing in the last year of Delia's life. No longer did her mother seem to object to her very presence. Unfortunately, Delia's death came before real healing between the two and Leona felt robbed of the mother/daughter closeness she so desired.

As Leona's voice gave out and the tears began to flow, John held her and gently wiped her tears with his own handkerchief. In control again, Leona was astounded at all that she had expressed to John. Never had she trusted another to this level. Never had she told this story in such depth. Here was someone with true capacity for empathy. "I see that John has a genuine interest in my life," Leona thought to herself.

"Thank you, John, for being here for me. I feel truly blessed."

Leona then asked John about his visit with his family and began learning more about this man who was becoming so important to her.

The couple spent as much time as possible together sandwiched between Leona's busy schedule and the hard work that John was doing for her father. During this time Leona discovered much more about John and his family and came to respect this strong and amazing culture. She learned more of the buffalo hunts that kept John's people on the move between Canada and the United States.

"As I mentioned before, summers were spent following the herds making jerky and pemmican from the meat," John explained. When Leona asked about pemmican John said that it was made of mashed dry meat, dried chokeberries, sugar and grease and that it was a favorite among his people. Leona was fascinated to learn that in the fall, when the buffalo coats were the best, the families would go out again for skins and fresh meat. Camps would be made to spend the winter months. That John's French ancestry had brought with it the Catholic religion was welcome knowledge to Leona since she had also been brought up in this faith. She heard from John that priests would often be available to say Mass or perform marriages and that it was at such a camp in Cypress Hills, Manitoba, that John was born.

"My mother explained to me that the families did not stay long in one place and often hardships were endured. At times, buffalo were very hard to find, sometimes water as well," described John. Through it all, the stories John heard were of happy lives, families who depended on one another, celebrated with song and dance, and were grateful for the lives they led.

Leona was very pleased that religion was an important part of the Métis life and that often Jesuit missionaries were with the community and nightly prayer meetings were an important part of the culture. She felt that this common ground between them might build a strong bond.

"John, as different as your life and mine appears to be, I see that we have much in common. My church is important to me and I include prayers in my daily life. Do you still practice your faith?" asked Leona.

Leona was used to seeing John with a very serious expression on his face. Indeed, his usual demeanor pleased that part of Leona who tended to put aside feelings of frivolity and rarely laughed out loud but what she saw now troubled her. John's face had closed down and clearly this subject was not one he intended to visit and most probably one that brought John pain. This was the second time Leona could see that John was hurting during their discussions of his life.

"John, please forgive me for intruding on your personal feelings. Sometimes my mind pursues topics that should be left alone. I am so sorry."

Slowly, Leona observed in John the moment when he moved into a space of trust. "Leona, I will talk to you about my feelings. It has been a while since I have faced them and somehow I believe that you will accept me as I am. Please allow me to tell of our lives in Lewistown and perhaps you will understand why I have drifted from the religion of my parents."

John continued to describe the lives of the Métis and share how his family had ended up in Lewistown, Montana in 1880 when John was an infant. Leona learned that Antoine and Angelique, John's mother and father were one of 25 families who founded the town of Lewistown. The way in which the Ouellette's and many other Métis families ended up at this location was a tale that Leona begged John to continue to tell.

"The story of your culture and the movement of the bands of Métis across Canada and into the United States is fascinating to me. My life has been one of rootedness on this farm and to speak to someone who has traveled as your family has, and…" At this point Leona felt embarrassed that she had pressed John for such a lengthy story and her crimson downturned face said it all.

John gently put his hand under Leona's chin, raised it and said, "Of course, I will tell you my family's story. Do not feel ashamed. I admit it is unusual for one as you to show such interest in people who are generally thought of as so different, but I am beginning to see that you are someone whose mind must be fed. But let's take a break. I have something of my family to share with you," suggested John with a twinkle in his eyes.

The couple ended up in the lovely flower garden where the fragrance of the wild prairie roses filled the air and Leona's other labors of love were poking their heads above the ground. Leona explained that there would soon be sweet peas climbing the trellis and snapdragons, zinnias and poppies adding color to this garden space. Although Leona's time in her garden had to be cut short because of the heavy workload, this was a task that lightened her heart.

John's sharing turned out to be a locket which contained a small photo of his dear Mother inside. In addition, John brought out some pemmican, which his cousins had given him when he last visited the family, for Leona to taste. It was very different than anything she had tasted but she did enjoy the treat. Leona did not miss the meaning expressed with this gesture. Both the photo and the pemmican symbolized John's feelings about his family and sharing these with Leona was very meaningful to her.

Impulsively, Leona reached up and hugged John and thanked him for sharing his life with her.

John realized that Leona was becoming so important to him and he wanted to honestly communicate his thoughts, even though he found this difficult to do. "Leona, please do not take offense at this next part of my story, but we have not always been accepted by non-Indian people and although you and your father are not prejudiced, we have been hurt by others."

"Oh John, I truly want you to be honest with me about your feelings. I wish to understand."

John continued, "My father spoke often of the scarcity of the buffalo which led to our Métis bands migrating farther west following the rivers, hunting for our needs. And because of the hundreds of years of Métis travel between Canada and the United States, most hunting families had children born in both countries and did not necessarily live their lives on the side on which they were born. It was our way of life. Unhappily for us, with more white settlers, came difficulties. Lies were spread among white fur traders who felt we were taking their business and so called us illegal immigrants who should be chased back to Canada. There were often hurtful and untrue newspaper articles calling us half-breeds who rob white settlers. I tell you this Leona, my people are honest and hard-working and we made many attempts to find common ground with the white people. Some, like your father, are fair. Others consider us the lowest of people."

Leona's heart hurt for John and his people because she was beginning to see the unfair treatment of a noble race. Sliding her hand inside John's, Leona urged him to continue his story. She heard the pain in his voice when he described others who criticized the Métis way of life without really attempting to understand it. For example, the Métis were judged for being nomadic and not staying in one place, when like their Indian ancestors, following the food was part of the culture. In fact, the Métis would often build cabins and sometimes stay for several years.

Leona was so impressed with John's tale of the journey his family and their relatives made to Montana. Clearly his family had been proud of their lives and had shared the past with their children.

"Since this area looked like such a good land, my father and several other families applied for homesteads in 1879 and 80. A trading post was set up and cabins were built. My father was a very hard worker and he and others in the band built a community before long."

"John, you must have been just as curious as I about your ancestors. You seem to know a great deal."

"This is part of our culture. Stories from our grandparents included the travels and the customs that these travels were built around. My mother, Angelique, told of the Métis' interest in maintaining the traditional way of life while also attempting to learn the customs of the settlers who were slowly making their way into the Judith Basin. Something that was very important to my mother, particularly because she spoke some English, was that her children all speak this language. The band established a school right away and hired an English-speaking teacher. Our people knew the importance of the children learning skills, including English, so that we could prosper in this new community.

"That is why your speech is so easy for me to understand. I often hear some words that are unfamiliar to me and you have a definite French accent, but for the most part, you learned your lessons very well, "said Leona.

"Yes. When I was just a small boy we had a one room school house in which the Métis as well as some of the white children attended. I was very happy there. Sadly, much began to change over the years as more white settlers moved into the area. We had always been happy to live with all people but as I have explained, many of the settlers came with prejudices against us. As these businessmen took over more of the businesses, some of our people were pushed out. Many of our people spoke little English. We looked and dressed differently and with more and more white settlers there seemed to be many bad feelings toward us."

Each time John spoke of the displaced feelings he and his people faced, Leona's heart broke a little more. For John and for his people, Leona was ashamed. John could see within her eyes an expression he did not often see when speaking to a non-Métis. It was one of understanding. If he thought for a moment pity was what Leona felt, he would not wish to continue with his story.

John put his arm around Leona and hugged her to him as he went on. "The Lewistown Métis families were landowners and considered prosperous, respected members of the community. In fact, some of our people gave freely to support places like the church. My father donated land for Lewistown's first cemetery. But it was not long until non-Métis settlers took over the Catholic parish. When I was 15, I do remember one priest, Father John van den Heuvel, who accepted our customs and spoke our language. He made many friends among our people. It was sad to see him go after 2 years with us. After that time, the church became a place where we felt separate and displaced."

"What changed within the church for you to feel so unwelcome?" asked Leona.

"Our families were encouraged to send their children to be educated at the mission schools. Our parents felt this would be a good move because in our schools with the increase in non-Métis settlers, we were often suffering from prejudiced feelings. But as I look back, I believe this was a point in our lives in Lewistown that led some of the young people, myself included, away from the church and from good feelings about ourselves."

Never having attended a mission school, Leona was anxious but a little afraid to hear what had happened to make John feel so sad but she encouraged him to continue to disclose this that lay so heavily on him.

"In the mission school, the Métis and Indian children were segregated from the white children. We had a separate area where we lived, studied, ate, and played and never with the other children. We were not allowed to speak anything but English. This was very hard on many whose families did not speak English. I was 12 at the time and had learned some English at my other school and from my mother. But many of the children were not that lucky."

"We spent more time in manual labor than in studying subjects that would help us get along in the world like arithmetic, reading, spelling, and geography. The education given the Métis children would not enable us to operate businesses or understand terms of bank loans or tax laws."

"Always our people were proud to call themselves Métis. At this school we began to lose some of that pride when we were identified as Indian. We did not have prejudice against the Indians, but being called such made us even more isolated from the white children. Our parents began to realize that we were not being educated well."

At this point, John looked vacantly across the prairie and stopped talking. Leona waited patiently and then asked, "You are remembering something that makes you very unhappy, aren't you John?"

"Yes, Leona, some of my memories are painful. One incident that I have so much trouble forgiving is when my sister received first communion at St. Peter's Mission school. At that event there were seven white girls who wore white dresses and thirteen "Indian" girls who wore pink. Mary wore pink. Mary was surprised to learn she was considered Indian because all her life her family were Métis in her eyes. The white girls and their parents were served lunch together while the Indian girls whose parents were not invited, ate lunch separately in the art room. Our parents, as devout Catholics, had always taught us to respect the priests and nuns, but it began to become very difficult to do this when we were being treated so harshly. It was here that we learned prejudice."

Leona began to truly understand that John and his community of Métis had felt the ache of gross injustices. "John, I cannot believe your sister and her friends were so blatantly mistreated. I am ashamed and reject this part of my culture. You will find that many people would agree with me."

Leona asked John about the Indian reservations she had heard of and whether he or his family were able to be part of that. John's face immediately grew solemn as he spoke,

"Leona, this is a subject which has hurt my people so much. We have never expected handouts and have been a hardworking and proud culture. However, our dealings with the government have brought sadness to our lives."

John told of a fellow Métis named Louis Riel who fought for Métis and Indian rights both in Canada and the United States. John related that his father and his older brothers and many others from the Lewistown band signed a petition written by Riel in 1880. It requested land, funds for schools, agricultural implements, seeds and animals. The idea was that the Métis would be given this start and then be self-supporting, not needing the annual provisions issued to Indians by the government. But John learned from his family that the Department of the Interior rejected the petition. John remembered his father's unusual reaction to this rejection. Usually a calm and peaceful man, Antoine's face turned crimson and his voice shook with anger as he shared this unjust treatment.

"Leona, my family continued to hope that they would be treated fairly. Another attempt to assist the Chippewa Indians and Métis was made by a Chippewa chief named Little Shell who pled with the government to set aside reservation land with good soil and hunting possibilities for the people. The government did not listen."

Instantly, Leona understood the deep pain and agony each of his family members must have felt. As she comforted John as best she could, Leona was heartsick that the government to which she had pledged her allegiance would treat these Native Americans as if they were intruders on the very land which they had treated with such reverence and respect.

John expressed, of course, just such a longing—to belong. Perhaps this fact as much as her attraction to John's dark, good looks and gentle maturity made Leona feel that they could have a future together. Leona's sharp mind began to wonder if she could be part of helping John heal from his experience with the church in Montana and so before giving it too much thought she asked, "John, I wonder if you might accompany me to church on Sunday. Father Fox at St. Joseph's Parish is a very loving man."

Leona held her breath and looked into John's eyes to see if she could determine his feelings. Slowly a welcome smile began to form on John's face and Leona knew she hadn't made a huge mistake after all. That Sunday the couple, with butterflies in their stomachs, attended St. Joseph's in Devil's Lake. The parishioners took some long looks at the two but in the end welcomed John and Leona.

One day soon after the visit to St. Joseph's, John took Leona's hand and asked her to sit with him under her favorite tree. "Leona," John began. "You know that your father's work for me is coming to an end and I have more work up north I must do."

Leona had dreaded this day and yet was aware it was coming. How she would miss this dear, sweet man whom she had become so attached to in such a short time. Leona knew, however, that there were many changes coming up in her life and that John had responsibilities he must attend to. With great reluctance, Leona opened her heart. "I confess, John, that I will miss you and our talks. You must know you have become very important to me but I know you must leave. In truth, my father tells me that since my mother's death, he no longer has the heart to continue on with the farm. He is planning to sell it this year and move into town. I will be assisting the move and setting up housekeeping wherever that ends up being."

John's next words brought Leona up short and she had to ask him to repeat them.

"What did you say, John?"

I said, "Keesha Kee Taen, I love you, Leona."

"When I return next year, I want you to marry me and come to Canada to live as my wife. I am considerably older than you and have little to offer you but a small cabin and my devotion to you. I have come to love you very much."

Leona felt so many emotions coursing through her she was at a loss for words. Fear was perhaps the foremost feeling immediately followed by amazement and wonder that John actually wanted to marry her. John watched Leona and wondered at the myriad of expressions he saw in this complex young woman's face. He began to worry that Leona was going to decline.

At 36 years of age, John had never married and not until he met Leona did he consider sharing his life with another. Perhaps he had misread Leona's interest in him and it was merely her curiosity in someone so different from herself. But John had shared so much of himself with Leona and felt closer to her than anyone in such a long time. Leona saw the puzzled look on John's face and wanted so to set his mind at ease but was unsure.

Leona's cautious personality led her to answer in a shaky voice. "John, I care for you so much. Will you give me a day to examine my feelings? This is such a big decision for me and I must have time so I can be certain this is the right step for both of us."

Although John's heart sank, he smiled at Leona and replied that he would expect no less from her. For you see, one of the many things John had come to love about Leona was her thirst for knowledge and her clear-headed problem solving. Impulsive she was not, and so John knew that this was how Leona needed to handle this situation.

"I will meet you here tomorrow and you can tell me of your decision," remarked John in a serious voice.

As Leona ran back into the house, she realized there had been few times in her 17 years that she had experienced such a combination of clashing emotions. The excitement of leaving the only home she had ever known was a thrilling prospect one moment and so anxiety producing in the next that her heart raced and her hands became cold and clammy. "What is happening to me?" thought Leona. "I do not behave this way!" In desperation, Leona confided in her best friend, Zada, who had planned to drop by that very afternoon to see Leona. In the end, if it hadn't been for Zada, one wonders whether Leona would have found the strength to accept John's proposal of marriage.

As it happened, Zada had recently become engaged to a childhood friend and was very happy. Leona had known both Zada and her fiancé, Thomas, and was not surprised when they announced their engagement some months ago. After all, they had grown up in the same area, their families had known one another for many years and they had so much in common.

When Leona examined Zada's situation and then her own, there really was no comparison. Leona had only known John for a relatively short time, had met no one from his family as yet, or any of his friends. John's entire background was fascinating to Leona but consisted of wildly differing customs, language and beliefs. On top of that the couple was to make their home in Canada where Leona had never traveled. The girls were chatting in Leona's bedroom when Leona imparted her news of the proposal and immediately followed it with a list of all the fears she had been storing in her mind. Zada looked into Leona's eyes, listened intently, and held Leona's shaking hands. When Leona had run out of breath and of reasons why she should not marry John, Zada's reply was,

"But do you love him, Leona?"

This question stopped Leona in her tracks but before she could analyze it further she replied with a serious and impatient tone, "Yes, of course I love John or I would not even be considering this huge step."

"Well then, that is your answer clear and simple—go with your heart for once in your life, miss "brilliant" mind!" exclaimed Zada with a grin as she pulled Leona from the bed on which they were sitting and began dancing her around the room.

Zada always was able to lighten Leona's heart and guide her away from her tendency to allow intellect to dictate her own feelings. In fact, it was easy to understand why Leona and Zada were such fast friends. One a somewhat flighty, easily influenced dreamer, the other fiercely independent and rooted so in the world of facts and figures. Together they provided balance for one another. There had been many a time when Leona had been instrumental in tempering Zada's impulsiveness with common sense and, as in this case, Zada was skilled in giving Leona permission to look within and examine her own heart. At last, feeling the burden lifting and the fears dissolving, Leona's smiling face told the story.

"Yes, I shall marry John. I would like to have time to help my father sell the farm and move into town, which is what he wants to do, so next spring would be a good time for the wedding if John agrees. I would love so much for you and Thomas to stand up for us?" asked Leona of her best friend.

Zada couldn't have been happier to accept and the two girls began making plans for Leona's trousseau. Since Leona had lost her mother the year before, Zada's older sister, Lilian, would join the girls in the wedding plans. Leona shared that her mother had worn a lovely while linen dress with covered buttons running the length of the dress for her wedding. Zada knew that Lilian would offer to alter the dress if need be. Although months away, the excited girls planned a dinner for the wedding party which would include the two couples and Leona's father and be hosted by Zada.

The next morning, Leona had approached her father before she told John she would marry him and asked what he thought. The conversation was lean, as was Lewis' way, and he cautioned Leona that the path might be difficult given that John was a Métis and society was often not accepting of his culture. He did, however, say he thought John an honest and hard-working man and gave Leona his blessing. Leona knew from Lewis' wistful look that he was wishing that his wife, Delia could be present. Leona wondered if any of John's relatives might attend the festivities.

The next afternoon Leona met John after his day's work. Again, John studied Leona's face trying to imagine what her words would be. All he saw there was a very serious Leona and he braced himself for her answer. "John I know I did not give you my answer to your proposal and you must be wondering. I believe I was so shocked that you wished to marry me that I couldn't even think. It took me a while to search my heart and soul and I now know that I very much want to be your wife. I dearly love you."

John looked into Leona's eyes and was much relieved after having experienced a fretful, sleepless night wondering if he had pushed Leona too quickly. "I was fearful that you would say, no, Leona," admitted John.

"But now I am a very happy man. The two embraced with the promise of sharing their lives together.

Leona told John of the plans that she and Zada had already made. John expressed an interest in traveling back to his cabin in Shaunavon, Saskatchewan, to make it ready for a wife. The details began to be ironed out and the date was set for April 24th in the year 1912.

Afterword

I enjoyed writing this portion of the story because it speaks of the relationship between Leona and the other characters. Developing connections with others is so important to me and it clearly showed up in this section. I examined the word "personality" and realized this term is one shared by our culture as a list of characteristics that make up a person's behaviors, general outlook on life and beliefs that have been passed down or developed as a result of life experiences. My understanding is that these attributes are really only a small part of the authentic being behind them. We are, in truth, ever so much more than a list of personality traits, even though we may not be conscious of this.

Nevertheless, I as the writer, and in large part the fiction writer, have examined my memories of Grandma Pearl aka Leona as the adult I knew and loved. From this perspective I have made assumptions that certain aspects of Grandma's personality that stood out to me were probably with her as a young girl. In addition, there are some letters and cards in my possession which gave me even a clearer view into this complex grandmother.

In building the relationship between Leona and her friend Zada, I am aware that I have used two distinct ways of viewing the world to form these characters. These two individuals moved through the world in completely different ways but were able to "complete" the other through friendship and respect. When Zada needed someone to bring her airy personality down to earth, Leona provided the grounding she needed. On the other hand, Leona tended toward becoming mired in her thoughts until she was unable to take action. Zada simply directed her to turn off her intellect long enough to recognize her feelings. Sometimes it takes another to remind us to listen to our inner self where we find the answers to what we only thought were problems. On a personal level I was taught to solve problems through examination, setting goals and working hard. The truth for me has become much simpler: listen to your heart and trust and the answers will come.

In forming my descriptions of Leona, I regret that I did not know Grandma in the last 20 years of my life. I long to sit with her and really listen to her heart, to get to know her on a deeper level. I would ask her of her feelings and spend time expressing the love that I have felt during the writing of this book. Thankfully, the letters that she wrote to my sister in later years gave me a small window into both the activities that gave her life purpose and the pain that made her life difficult.

My experience as both a granddaughter and a grandmother has taught me that there are some grandmas who are cuddlers and who revel in playing an active role in their grandchildren's lives. There are others who clearly love their grandchildren but are more aloof and wait to be invited. Grandma Pearl, in my eyes, fit the second definition. However, as I say this, I realize that my older sister, of 15 years, might have a completely different view. My younger sister and I were a second family, if you will, and Grandma was older and less active by the time we came along. In addition, my busy life did not include Grandma as I wish it had. In any event, one can see how my perspective is all I have and therefore wrote from that.

In my version of Grandma's life, the fact that she was in a home of Irish farmers left her feeling that she did not belong. One wonders if on some level her German ancestry as well as her mother's moodiness, contributed to these dissonant feelings. In fact, after Grandma discovered her true roots, she wrote a letter which stated that now she understood why she did not feel the love she thought should be available to her and that she felt the early experience of losing both her mother and her father left her "very neurotic." This neurosis did show itself, at least in later life, when Grandma was nervous and had sleeping problems.

Often, I contemplate how different Grandma's life might have been had her mother and father raised her. Clearly, Grandma carried confusion and pain as a result of her difficult life with Delia. Mary would have offered loving acceptance to her precious daughter, Pearl.

In this section, I included a great deal of my research about the Métis. I became keenly interested in the life of my grandfather and his ancestors. I identified with their strong kinship ties and love of family. I suspect that Grandma's curiosity and love of learning, as well as her confusing feelings toward her own family and the resulting and possibly unconscious search for connection and love in her life, would have been a large part of her fascination with John. Grandma's intellect would push her to discover what she could about this dark stranger and to be drawn to the many facets of his heritage. I can see her becoming passionate about events that were clearly not fair and right. Since Grandma saw things as black and white, right and wrong, she would have been a loyal and compassionate mate for John.

The following history of the Métis in general and my ancestors, the Ouellette family, in particular, should give the reader a more comprehensive view of life as it was for this culture. I include it because these experiences have also been my experiences—these "ones" are part of me.

Additional history of the Métis, the Ouellette family and its kin.

The pertinent history of the Métis was a fascinating chronicle of these ancestors which led me to a feeling of close connection to and compassion for my Grandfather Ouellette. John, at the age of two, became a part of the settling of a town in central Montana, Lewistown, on the tributaries of Spring Creek. This band of Métis are referred to as the Spring Creek or Lewistown Métis.

According to my genealogical study, many of John's ancestors came from the Red River Settlement in eastern Canada in what is now Manitoba. I discovered that the history of the fur trade is tied to the development of the Métis, or mixed blood people. A mobile economy, first based on the beaver and then the buffalo, resulted in the Métis eventually becoming valuable employees of the North-West and the Hudson's Bay Trading Companies. Intermarriage between the Chippewa Indian women, whose knowledge and skills contributed to the success of the fur trade, and the French fur traders and company men became the basis of the Métis culture with its strong kinship ties.

Over time, as game became less plentiful along the Red River, Métis families conducted large scale and distant hunts traveling from Canada to places in the United States. These Métis bands spent summers following the herds making pemmican from the meat and in the fall going out for fresh meat and buffalo robes. Families would travel and hunt together. They visited back and forth between the U.S. and Canada and maintained these kinship ties. Trading posts, such as Pembina where the Missouri and Red Rivers meet, sprung up where the Métis could trade their buffalo robes and other furs. By the early 1800's there was a church and school there served by a Catholic Priest.

The Bottineau family (My Great Grandmother Angelique's maiden name) and the Ouellette family had a long association in the fur trade of the Red River and upper Missouri Rivers, North Dakota, and later on the plains of Montana where they organized their economic life around the buffalo. In North Dakota, near the Canadian border, there remains a town of Bottineau named after this well-known family. The town of Pembina, also in North Dakota, was the place at which John's mother, Angelique Bottineau, and his father, Antoine Ouellette, were married in 1857.

It was unfortunate that as the Métis culture developed and the bands traveled between the United States and Canada, the race prejudice intensified in both countries. The Métis, due to biracial backgrounds, were especially judged. Their "nomadic" habits were often criticized and they were considered indolent. That these people were peaceful and hardworking with a family structure and unique culture in language, dress, and music which was borrowed from French, Scottish, Chippewa, Cree and other groups was rarely appreciated. Here we have a case of misunderstanding and fear of people who exhibited a different way of life.

An example of the many intelligent methods used by the bands of related Métis is that they found it useful to select leaders who could speak some English as well as the Métis language, Michif, and a number of Indian languages. They could negotiate the right to hunt and trade on traditional Indian land. In this way some of the disagreements between whites, Indians, and Métis could be settled peacefully.

In the mid 1800's, as the population of the Pembina River area grew and there was pressure to enforce border regulations, the U.S. government initiated treaty negotiations and proposed that Indians and Métis be put on reservations. Unfortunately, neither interested Indian parties, recognized Chippewa leaders, nor Métis were allowed to participate. In fact, the Métis were excluded based on the belief that they were unqualified. In many cases, Indians were settled on reservations but their Métis relatives were required to provide evidence of their citizenship and European ancestry and were then offered land which was physically separated from their Indian relatives.

This situation worsened because of confusion as to the rights of the Métis as individuals. Even though in the government's eyes Métis were not considered Indian, and therefore unable to become enrolled members of a tribe assigned to a reservation, their association with Indians in the minds of both U.S. and Canada led officials to deny them basic liberties. Not recognized as Native people, they received no rations to help them get through the winter. Nor were they given protection from, or compensation for, any Indian attacks they may have faced.

As the band followed the buffalo, John's family stopped in Cypress Hills in Canada where John was born in 1878. The Spring Creek band then traveled to Montana along the Milk River. The men would hunt, buy supplies from traders who traveled with the bands, and the women would do all the tanning of the buffalo hides and make the jerky meat, pemmican, and moccasins just as they had for many years.

Fortunately for the Spring Creek band of which John's relatives were a part, as the army was stepping up their program to expel Canadian Métis and as the number of buffalo in the area declined, the Métis bands were starting to break up and move away. In early May 1879 some of the Spring Creek band traveled from the Milk River to Fort Benton, where they crossed the Missouri River by ferry. A military escort accompanied them to what is present day Lewistown. In August, the Antoine Ouellette and Edward Wells families crossed the Missouri by ferry and joined relatives on Spring Creek. Here a substantial party in which all the families were closely related settled.

In the story John related to Leona, he mentioned the attempt to assist the Chippewa Indians and the Métis by Chief Little Shell. This was in 1892 when John Bottineau, a relative of Angelique's' and a prominent North Dakota lawyer, assisted Chief Little Shell in trying to negotiate a treaty with the U.S government over what is now the Turtle Mountain Indian Reservation. It was known as the "Ten Cent Treaty" because the government purchased one million acres at the rate of only ten cents per acre. The area set aside by the government for a reservation was untillable. The tribe objected to that, as well as the very low settlement amount, but were unsuccessful in improving the situation. As a result of their agitation, Chief Little Shell and his followers, together with John Bottineau, were driven off the Turtle Mountain Reservation. The end result was that the government cut the size of the reservation and removed many families from the rolls.

John told of the difficulties the Spring Creek Métis met while settled in Lewistown. The disappearance of the buffalo had overwhelming consequences as the loss of this livelihood was realized for many Métis. Fortunately for the Spring Creek population the community continued to grow. At one time 150 Métis families were present. By 1893 the influx of Euro-Americans in the community brought an end to the Métis' economic control. Both the Métis and their Indian relatives confronted increasing discrimination and they lost influence in the institutions that they helped create.

The Spring Creek families felt the impact of the homestead boom and the railroads. Those families who had secured homesteads continued to farm and to supplement their incomes with a variety of jobs in the community including: housemaids, freighters, miners, farmhands and day laborers. Still, the families maintained a kin-based society even if their homes were located as far away as fifty miles north and east of Lewistown.

My research left me appreciating the noble culture of the Métis and feeling the pain of their challenges. I felt most proud of their continual ability to adapt to changing times and maintain their distinct identities, centering their lives on strong kinship ties and a sense of community. Always the hope for John and Leona was that they could maintain their identities as they embarked upon a new community experience in Shaunavon.

Little Leona (Pearl)

Leona at 14, left, and a niece of Lewis Brys

Red River Cart

Fur Traders

Buffalo Hunt Caravan

Pembina Post Office, 1863

Métis Dance

Old Time Fiddle

Lewistown Settlement

Angelique Bottineau

Lucy Ouellette, Alexina Wells Ouellette (mother), Matthew (baby), Lena Ouellette, Frank Ouellette (father)

Chapter 3

It had been a very busy year for Leona and Lewis. The prospective bride missed John but fortunately had many activities that kept her from feeling too lonely. Her father had been successful selling the homestead and had found a job in town at the livery. He had always enjoyed working with horses and so the position was a Godsend for this man who needed to start anew. The search for a new home had been relatively easy as a member of the church had decided to move back east and rented Lewis a small home very near town.

Leona busied herself making curtains for the windows and setting up the kitchen area so her father would be comfortable when she and John were married in the spring. She looked at each of the domestic duties as practice for the time when she would be the mistress of her own cabin in Shaunavon. The prospect was a little daunting to this girl who had spent her whole life in North Dakota. Given Leona's personality, she wished to know in detail what the future held.

"Perhaps this is a lesson for me that I have to let go of always knowing the next step in my life," mused Leona.

One activity that helped Leona feel some sense of control, was stocking her hope chest with more of the items she imagined the couple would need in their home. Realizing that this had been a single man's cabin, she imagined there were many basic things that might be missing. Before Delia passed away, she foresaw a future for Leona and John and so encouraged Leona to begin filling the trunk. As mother and daughter worked together on the sewing and embroidering, they developed a closeness that was new to the relationship.

Leona was grateful that she had had this time with Delia before her death. As she gently folded the bedding she had acquired and placed it in the trunk, and examined some of the pillow slips that Delia had embroidered, she was able to feel kindness, if not love, for this woman who had raised her. Their previous history made it difficult for Leona to build a strong connection with Delia, but now Leona, as a young adult about to embark on her own married life, felt able to let go of the past and be glad for the change in her own heart.

Before long, Leona began to see signs of spring in this prairie community. The birds were singing, the prairie flowers were beginning to open up, and the damp and cold of winter dissipated. How Leona loved this time of year. "Especially this year!"

John and Leona had exchanged letters and information concerning his arrival in North Dakota and Lewis' new address. Leona's letter was filled with her excitement to see her soon-to-be husband as well as the plans she and her friend Zada had made for the wedding and the dinner afterwards. As she reread her letter before sending it, Leona wondered about this man who had asked her to marry him. "Is he as excited as I am to begin this new life or is it just the woman's place to feel these feelings?" As these thoughts came to her, Leona scolded herself for these unexpected sentiments which sounded too much like her friend Zada and not like practical Leona. "I must forgive myself. After all, this is my marriage and perhaps a little emotion is to be expected." Leona's heart was opening.

Before long it was the day Leona was to meet John at the train station. She had asked her father to hitch up the horse to the wagon. In the meantime, Leona dressed with care and was soon on her way to the station. The excited young woman was just approaching her destination when she heard a long whistle, saw the steam of the train in the distance, and knew that soon she would be with her betrothed. Quickly, she tied up the horse and wagon and ran to meet John as he was climbing down the stairs of the train.

Upon seeing her handsome fiancé, Leona stopped in her tracks and began to worry lest he think her unladylike if she didn't calm herself. But once Leona observed John's wide smile, she gained confidence and literally danced into his arms. The two kissed and held each other as only a couple can that have been separated for these many months. The desire felt by John and Leona warmed these two young people and only Leona's sense of propriety at behaving like this in a public place allowed her to gently push John away.

"I have missed you!" exclaimed John.

"And I you!" agreed Leona.

And just like that, the two began talking as if no time at all had passed since they had last been together. The ride back was filled with the longing of each to begin their new lives. With scarcely a week before the wedding, Leona began to fill John in on more of the wedding plans which included a visit to the priest.

"And then we will exchange rings and the ceremony will be over," chattered Leona—again in that uncharacteristic way.

"Well, it certainly is a good thing I made a plan for a ring for you," teased John.

Realizing her presumption, Leona looked shyly at John and asked, "You did?"

"I have a ring that was my Grandmother's and I will be very pleased to place it on your finger in one week's time," replied John.

Leona was happy that John recognized some of the traditions that were dear to her. Others that had not been part of his cultural upbringing were welcomed by John in his open and accepting way. Clearly, John wished to please his bride as much as she wanted John to be comfortable and happy. Leona trusted John but still worried that her wedding night would somehow be a disappointment to him. Fortunately Leona was able to admit her feelings to Zada who shared that she had had some of the same concerns herself before her wedding night. "Trust John to guide you and be honest with him about your trepidations," were the words lovingly expressed with this nervous girl soon to share a bed with a much older man.

The day before the wedding the two met with the priest to have a discussion about the couple's religious beliefs and about raising children in the church. John was willing to let go of his resentful feelings toward the church in order that Leona's wedding day be all she desired.

The day had arrived. All the necessary people had assembled. The bride and groom had made themselves ready and the ceremony was about to begin. In the seats of the small Catholic Church which Leona and her family had attended were neighbors and friends who wished to join the happy event. Zada's husband, Thomas, had offered to stand up for John and so the two were waiting in the front of the church with the priest for the bride to join them. The young men were so handsome in their suits and ties. However, on John's forehead appeared the sheen of perspiration and he felt his knees quaking. But Thomas, newly married himself, assured John that he would get through this event fairly unscathed.

With the sound of the sweet melody of The Wedding March being played by the church's pianist, John felt his heart begin to race as his bride approached with her father, Lewis, whose smile helped to calm John's frazzled nerves. To John, Leona was beautiful.

Fortunately, the ceremony was short and as Leona and John exchanged wedding bands, they promised their commitment to one another. Leona felt honored to have been gifted a ring worn by John's maternal grandmother and she knew she would treasure it always. Her father had helped Leona select a plain gold band for John. After the vows, the rings, and the kiss, the couple turned toward their guests and were accepted as Mr. and Mrs. John Ouellette.

Afterwards, the bridal party posed for a photo: Thomas and John, Zada and Leona lovely in their linen dresses. The girls had spent much time tying each other's hair with silken ribbons while Zada's ready laughter and lightheartedness had calmed Leona's nerves.

Lilian, Zada's sister, served a delicious lemon cake and lemonade was available in delicate crystal cups. Everyone congratulated the couple and much to Lewis' relief, he saw no signs of disapproval of the marriage. "At least in our circle of friends there is no discrimination for Leona and John to experience," thought Lewis.

The wedding dinner was a lovely event. Lilian and her husband Waliaw joined the party and there was much laughter and fun. Lewis had been told of John and Leona's plans to travel to Shaunavon where John owned a cabin to begin their married life. He wished to send them off on their journey with a small nest egg and presented it to the couple at the dinner party.

"I thank you sir. Your generosity is greatly appreciated," remarked John with that solemn look that spoke of his sincerity. "This entire day has been a revelation to me! So many have extended such caring and wished us so well on this day. My only regret is that some of my family could not be here. Thank you all."

Leona understood what it took for John to make such a declaration and she loved him even more. The love the happy couple shared was demonstrated with just a look and a smile from each. They joined hands and felt blessed at this moment.

Next Zada and Thomas presented their gift to the newlyweds: a night's stay at the new hotel in town which would include a hearty breakfast before the couple began the journey up north. Her Father was to pick them up at the hotel in the morning and take them to the train station. Leona was so looking forward to their stop in Qu'Appelle, Saskatchewan, where Antoine, John's father and Odilon, his brother, lived. At last Leona would meet some of the family with whom she already felt an unexpected kinship as a result of the loving descriptions and obvious closeness John felt for his family.

That evening, alone in the couple's hotel room, Leona nervously prepared herself for her first night with her new husband. Zada had sewn a beautiful nightgown for this special night. As Leona slipped the silky creation over her head she remembered more of Zada's words. "This is the time of joining with the man who holds your heart. Do not be afraid and more than that, allow yourself to treasure being loved by John." When John gently knocked on the room door and entered after hearing Leona's, "Come in," the loving look from John's eyes was all Leona needed to feel she could happily take Zada's advice. "Oh how I love this man."

On the morning of their departure Leona's heart fluttered with a combination of excitement and nerves. Never having left her North Dakota area, this was to be a big adventure. Sorry to leave her father and her friends, Leona was ready to be the wife of this beloved man. John had proven to be a sensitive and generous lover and Leona was even more devoted to her husband. As the train drew in to the station, Leona hugged her father and thanked him for everything, including the lunch which he so generously had packed for them. Feeling that curious mixture of emotions, Leona followed John as he climbed the steps of the train and entered the Pullman car in which they would find their seats for the journey to Qu'Appelle.

Leona found the swift movement of the train and the surrounding countryside a wonderful experience, notwithstanding the noise from the engine and the warm environment resulting from the steam. Leona found that the prairie in Canada was not too different from the one in which she was raised. She enjoyed seeing the prairie grasses, scattered cattle, and sparsely placed sod houses and cabins. John's brother, Odilon, had agreed to meet the train when it arrived in Qu'Appelle. From there the couple would be taken by cart and horse for a short ride to the homestead.

As the train moved along, Leona's mind was filled with questions. In her education and in her own household, it was a given belief that the country had blessed its citizens with much to be grateful for. Certainly at the time her father moved to North Dakota from Duluth in 1895, he had been given an opportunity when the government provided a homestead to those willing to work the land and grow a prosperous community in the plains states. Throughout Leona's schooling, she was taught that there were equal opportunities for all which came from the democratic government, its elections and laws to protect all.

However, now that Leona had heard of John and his family's history, she was very confused. She began to examine the sequence of events that led to John's displaced feelings. John's father and others who had made the journey to Montana in 1879 applied for homesteads and were given them. This was not unlike the experience of Leona's father. They worked the land, built a school and began to prosper. It sounded to Leona as if they were very hard working, family folks who for many years were able to continue with these traditions no matter where they made their home.

When they reached Montana, they truly felt as if they were ready to make this community one in which to raise their children and live a contented life.

Leona was reminded of the story told by John that as more white settlers came into the area, aspects of life clearly became more difficult for the Ouellettes and other Métis in the community. The government convinced the parents to send their children to mission schools which unfortunately taught the lesson that they were not equal to white children and therefore did not deserve the same education. Louis Riel attempted to improve their cause when he filed a petition with the Department of Interior which would have resulted in the Métis becoming more self-supporting. That was denied. When Chief Little Shell attempted to intervene with the government in order to make reservation life more inclusive, the results were the exact opposite and many were denied. "Perhaps I have been very naïve to believe that this country truly welcomes all," thought Leona.

Leona wondered at a government that was presumably set up to include all within its borders with equal rights when clearly in many ways this was not the case for Métis or many Native Americans. While on this train of thought, Leona also wondered that women had not yet been given the right to vote. Leona knew that her studies and knowledge were equal to or better than many men in her community, although she would be ill advised to make such a statement out loud!

"My goodness!" Leona mused. "My mind has certainly been busy ruminating." Leona looked over to see that John had taken a nap. He looked relaxed and peaceful and the serious expression so often apparent had smoothed out. She wondered where they were and how long they had been on their journey when she heard the train whistle blow. John stirred and looked at Leona with a smile.

"Where are we, John?" asked Leona, never having taken this trip before. John checked his pocket watch and realized they had been on the trip for about four hours and were pulling into a station where the two of them would be able to get out, use the bathrooms and stretch their legs before boarding for another ten hours to reach their destination. Since the couple had left by 7:00 that morning their stop in Qu'Appelle where John expected his brother, Odilon, to meet would not be until about 9:00 that night.

Once they were back in their seats, Leona pulled out the basket her father had prepared for them. She found freshly baked bread, cheese, and potato salad along with a jar of lemonade. Canned preserves, dried meat, and delicious cake left over from the wedding rounded out the meal. Leona knew that her father had enlisted Zada and her sister Lilian's help with the lunch. They ate hungrily and still had plenty left to snack on before their journey's end.

"John, how long has it been since you have seen your father and brother?"

"I was visiting with family in Montana before I came to work with your father last year. My mother passed away in 1903, my father had moved to Qu'Appelle, but some of my sisters and brothers were still making their homes in Montana. Frank, my older brother had settled in Valley, Montana, near the Saskatchewan border. Father and Odilon traveled there to visit and we all stayed with Frank and Alexina, his wife and their children Lena, Lucy, Matthew, and baby Tony.

It was a happy time to be with the children and of course to visit with my brothers. We reminisced about the good times and the bad, sad that Mother could not have been with us."

"How old was your mother when she died, John?"

John did not answer immediately but gazed solemnly out the window for a moment before he said, "She did not live nearly long enough and I miss her every day. My mother was such a strong individual, always finding ways to keep the family together and remembering the strengths of our heritage. In a true Métis family there is a balance between the Indian ways and the French. Mother was the keeper of our Indian customs. Our religious beliefs were a combination of two worlds."

John stopped talking for a moment and exclaimed, "Leona, I have never met anyone like you. You can get me talking about things I rarely

71

think about. I did not even answer your question about my mother's age at the time of her death but I went on and on!"

Leona noticed that twinkle in John's eyes. Oh how she loved seeing this expression! It told her how much he really enjoyed sharing with her.

"Mother was only 65. I imagine having the number of children she had was not easy. Fifteen children by the time she was 50 took much energy. But she seemed to always have time for each of us. Keeping her family connected was very important. We all loved the times our community would get together. This would always involve music and dancing and delicious food the women would make. We kids would compete in our dancing because as the fiddling tempo increased so did the fancy footwork we added to our steps. Sometimes the men would play harmonicas, hand drums, and finger instruments like bones and spoons to tap out the rhythm and lead us in singing some of the traditional Métis songs. We kids would often drum on tin pans in time to the music. I miss that part of our lives in Lewistown."

"Perhaps you could share with me what some of your favorite foods are and I will learn to cook them. Since my mother died, and also the time I've spent this year taking care of Father, I have become quite handy in the kitchen. I feel I could learn what I need to please you," remarked Leona.

"I'm sure whatever you cook will be just right," said John as he winked at his new bride. "All of us kids did love the meat pie, bannock, steamed pudding, and custard that mother made for us. Pemmican was another treat we didn't always have but enjoyed. Mother would make it from either dried buffalo or venison. Whenever Father took some of us hunting, we would pack some pemmican in our animal-hide bags and it would provide us with an easy treat. After we returned with game from the trip, Mother's reverence for the animals was apparent. She taught us the First Peoples connection to the earth and all that inhabited it. I always treasured what Mother brought from her heritage."

"I love hearing about ideals that your family held onto. As far as cooking goes, I can't promise you the pemmican but surely I can handle the pudding and custard. What exactly is bannock, John?"

"Bannock is bread like fry bread. It can be baked in an oven, cooked in a skillet over a fire, or fried. It was easy to make and even I would try my hand at it. It was especially practical because it lasted a long time without spoiling and was very filling. In fact, I have been on my own for some time and you may be surprised to know that I have learned to cook for myself!"

"Wonderful," exclaimed Leona. "You can teach me and join me in the cooking! I wonder, did your mother also sew for the household?"

John answered an emphatic, "Yes!" and then told Leona about the beautiful beadwork that his mother put on the jackets, leggings, gloves and vests that she made for the family. Leona learned that the beads were actually seeds and were sewn on in a floral pattern. "This was a tradition Mother was taught by her grandmother, Marguerite. The women became known as the "Flower Beadwork People" and this was a sign of pride for them. Mother used tanned animal skins or sometimes cloth to make all of our clothes. My sisters learned embroidery at the mission school and they began to also make very handsome floral designs for our clothing. Mother also made a variety of sizes of birch bark baskets, some of which she gave to me and are stored in my cabin."

"I enjoy sewing so I can keep you in shirts and pants. But sewing on leather might be beyond my talents. I am willing to try anything, John. Although I have never made a basket, I am anxious to see your Mother's creations. In our family, perhaps we can find that same balance that your mother and father seemed to have in their marriage. Compromise is a good thing and again I am very willing to put in the effort to help you keep some of those memories that warm your heart."

John gently lifted Leona's chin and kissed her. No more needed to be stated. Each of these gentle souls was perhaps stepping beyond their comfort zone but in love, all things were possible. That was the feeling that permeated the space in which John and Leona traveled that day so long ago.

After several more stations, John remarked that they were nearly at their destination. Leona again felt a similar "butterflies in the stomach" feeling that she had experienced at the start of their journey. At last she would meet some of John's family. Would they like her? Would she fit in? Leona understood she would be the only woman in this household. "Now quit borrowing trouble," Leona thought to herself. "I must view this as an adventure and not a tooth extraction!"

"Are you all right?" asked John with a concerned look on his face. Clearly he had noticed that Leona was fidgeting and had lost all the color in her face. "Are you ill?"

"No, John. I am just being silly worrying about whether your family will accept me."

John assured her that one of his father's most appealing traits included his acceptance of all people. "Remember the story I told you about my father and the rest of the Spring Creek band first settling in Lewistown? Well, as white settlers came into the area, father was always the first one to welcome them and to offer any assistance they might need. Many people were happy to meet him but as you know, others were resistant to someone they saw as different from them."

"I am sure that my mind is just leading me on a fearful path and I intend to stop it right now!" Leona declared with a very serious expression.

Leona and John heard the whistle announcing the station and felt the train slow down. Tired and bones creaking, they were both happy to end the journey on this day. As they exited the train, each of them carrying bags, John announced that his brother, Odilon, was approaching. A smiling gentleman who did not have the same Métis features as his brother, held his hand out to Leona. "I have been told your name is Leona and I am very happy to be meeting you this evening."

John was impressed by the welcoming and open face of his brother and teasing as brothers do, John grabbed Odilon in a headlock and growled, "You better be pleased to meet her because this is my wife!"

The brothers ended their momentary wrestling with a hug between two obviously loving family members and Odilon asked if there was more luggage to claim. Leona described a trunk in the train car and Odilon and John retrieved it. "Our buggy is parked in the back of the station so follow me," requested John's younger brother. The tired couple followed along, John helping Odilon with the trunk. The buggy contained plenty of room for the three adults and they stowed their luggage in the back. It was a short ride to the homestead but Leona found herself leaning against John and dozing on and off. It was as if her eyes could take in no more this day and sleep was necessary.

Odilon noticed how tired Leona looked and quickly parked the buggy in front of the cabin. "Why don't you each take your carpet bags and I will get the trunk later after I've shown you inside to your room. I know how exhausting a long journey can be and if I'm not mistaken you had many festivities yesterday which probably wore you out."

Leona was so grateful to this thoughtful man! She followed him inside a handsome log cabin. Odilon explained that his father, Antoine, had gone to bed and that since there were just two bedrooms, he and his father would share a room for the time John and Leona were visiting.

"Thank you so much for your hospitality, Odilon. We have had a long journey and although our wedding and dinner afterwards were perfect, I'm afraid I am bushed," said Leona sleepily. John agreed and the couple settled in to their spartan bedroom and were soon sound asleep.

Birds chirping outside the window brought Leona awake and she noticed John was not beside her. Definite male voices could be heard in the other room and Leona quickly dressed, combed her hair, and made ready to meet John's father. With a smile on her face, Leona refused to give in to fears about this meeting.

"Good morning sleepyhead!" remarked John when Leona entered the kitchen where preparations were being made for breakfast. "Father, I am very happy to introduce you to my wife, Leona."

"Oh, now I see where Odilon got his European features," thought Leona. A handsome, mustached gentleman stood up to greet Leona. "How happy we are that you have stopped to visit us here in Qu'Appelle. Welcome, Leona, to a small part of the family. I hope that you will meet others as time goes on."

"I am so happy to be here as well. John has told me much about your family and I am eager to learn more."

"Yes, John shared with us at our last visit that he was very taken with a young lady who asked countless questions and showed such interest in our family. I am impressed that you apparently got John to open up and share with you. He has always been the quiet, thoughtful son." With this comment, Leona saw a twinkle in Antoine's eyes that made her feel at such ease and the recurring butterflies were let go and replaced with an emotion she had difficulty naming but felt very fine indeed.

"Yes, Mr. Ouellette, I am very much interested in your very different but appealing heritage. John's stories leave me wondering at the experiences you and your family have had. My life, by comparison, seems so mundane." Leona reminded herself that she would not be bringing up any of the events that had occurred in John's life and had so troubled him.

"Well, Leona," replied Mr. Ouellette. "First of all, I would very much like you to call me Antoine if you wouldn't mind. I rarely think of myself as Mr. Ouellette these days! And concerning our heritage, there is nothing we like better than to share our family's fine adventures. I am only sorry you did not come along in John's life in time to meet my wife, Angelique. She truly was the keeper of the family's history."

"Yes, John mentioned that very fact on the train ride here."

Leona was very taken with this distinguished looking gentleman. For the few days they would be visiting with John's family, Leona knew she would enjoy getting to know both Odilon and Antoine but also this country north of her home in North Dakota. Leona smiled her thanks as

Odilon placed bowls of oatmeal, a plate of biscuits and honey and hot coffee on the table in front of her. There was rich milk from their cow as well. She realized then just how hungry she was!

That day John and Leona saddled up two horses from the barn so John could show his wife around this part of Saskatchewan. On the way to the barn they visited the garden which was much like the one she had worked at home. Small buds could be seen breaking through the earth ready to soak up the spring sunshine. The couple rode for several miles, enjoying the breeze on this lovely spring day. Leona spotted the beautiful orange prairie lily, bright sunflowers, and yellow cornflowers which added color to the prairie grasses.

"I was so tired, John, when we pulled into the train station last night, I didn't even look around at the town. Is there much to see?" asked Leona.

"This town has grown in the last few years. We'll ride that direction, tie up our horses and you can see for yourself."

Leona was surprised to see the size of Qu'Appelle and the extent of the buildings in town. Compared to her hometown, this was a thriving metropolis! After tying up the horses, the couple walked down wooden sidewalks and saw the library, bank, and hotel. The brick town hall was large and imposing and Leona was interested in the architectural style of it. The Queen's Hotel seemed very grand to her as well. The couple continued through town and passed the feed store, harness shop, and livery.

"I'm feeling a little like a country bumpkin the way I've been gawking at this fine town," remarked Leona. When they reached the Post Office, Leona mentioned that she would like to write a letter home to Father and Zada and now she knew just where to mail them. Fortunately, Leona had seen fit to tuck some stationery in her bag so she could stay in touch with her loved ones.

Before the couple left town, they stopped in the general store and picked up some provisions for the time they would be visiting. Again, Leona noticed that the items available surpassed those she could find in their small town of Albert, North Dakota. The trip back enabled Leona to see more of the lovely spring prairie and the small ranches and dwellings of other folks who had also made their home in this area.

Another day, Antoine brought out a photograph of his wife that had been taken when they lived in Lewistown and was a larger version of the locket photo John had shared with Leona. Leona marveled at the resemblance John had to his mother, whose looks spoke of the First People as John had described them. Although part French herself according to John, Angelique did not seem to take after that side of her family.

One evening, Leona was gifted with Odilon's fine playing on the fiddle he had made himself. Antoine and John accompanied him on harmonicas. The music was lively and Leona was soon clapping her hands and tapping her feet to the beat. At one point, John and Antoine sang a plaintive sounding song that somehow made Leona feel sad even though, since it was in French, she recognized few of the words. Afterwards, Antoine explained that it was in fact a song of remembrance because it was describing the Métis defeat at the battle of Batoche and the resulting execution of Louis Riel whom Métis looked to for leadership at difficult times in Métis history.

"John told me a great deal about your history but I don't think we discussed this battle. Where is Batoche?" asked Leona.

"It is about 250 miles from Qu'Appelle more in the middle of Saskatchewan," answered John.

Antoine began to describe the meaning of the words of the song in more detail. He explained that both he and Angelique and many of their relatives had been born and lived east of Saskatchewan in Red River Settlement, which was called Rupert's Land at that time.

"Our families had land which we farmed when we were not traveling to follow the buffalo. Many of us worked for the Hudson's Bay Company, trading furs for our needs. I remember my father and mother speaking of this as a good life for the Métis until the government and new settlers to the area began to make changes that were not in our best interests," Antoine explained with a sober expression.

Antoine continued to explain the complicated circumstances which drove the Métis from their homes.

"Canada annexed the land on which we had lived for many years without consulting any of the Métis. Our leader, Louis Riel, led the Métis in resisting this annexation and was able to get the government to sign The Manitoba Act which created the new province of Manitoba. Unfortunately, life was not the same in our Red River settlement and many of us left to find other suitable land on which to make our homes, still following the buffalo as our major source of existence," remarked Antoine.

"I am telling you this long tale because it predates the Batoche resistance but is connected in so many ways to our history. In 1885, no one asked the Métis or First Nations how they would like to see the West developed. There were many prejudices against our language, our religion, our culture. People did not understand that we were trying to maintain our way of life."

Antoine continued, "General Middleton was sent with his forces to the village of Batoche. It was clear that the government had sent their army to remove the Métis from our land. We knew that they needed land for their railroad and that giving us fair value for ours was never going to happen. The Métis decided to take a stand against this. Unfortunately, the Métis were outnumbered four to one and although they fought bravely, were defeated. After the battle, many were dead, including my father, Joseph Ouellette. My uncle Moise fought but survived. The women and children were hidden in the bushes or caves where the young children's voices would not be heard. They had to cook their food at night so their fires would not be seen. It was a frightening time for them.

Our songs often carry the history of the Métis so we can remember that we are a proud and noble people who chose to fight for our families and the rights we deserved. Although we were not successful, we are not ashamed of what we did."

Leona was amazed at the strength of this culture to have continued surviving and thriving despite the many obstacles to their peaceful existence. She felt much sorrow for them and yet she could see that Antoine was not one to hold onto the pain but chose to rise above it and continue with pride. Now Leona could see the wisdom in moving his family to Montana where they were able, at least for a time, to prosper.

"Thank you, Antoine for sharing these stories with me. How heart breaking! I admire the choices the Métis have made."

"Thank you, Leona and thank you for marrying my son. I hope you will be very happy," answered Antoine with a sincere and genuine tone in his voice.

John had said little but the brightness of his eyes and the slight smile accompanied with a squeeze of Leona's hand spoke for him.

After the serious conversation, Antoine asked the brothers to show Leona the Red River jig while he played along on the fiddle. It was a lively tune and the seriousness of the previous moments was replaced with the music and the competition between the boys as they moved their feet as fast as Antoine was playing. Before long John pulled Leona out of her chair and the three of them were dancing, Leona trying her best to keep up with the movements. She thought she'd never laughed so hard, nor felt so at peace as she did in this little cabin on this spring evening.

Both Odilon and John began talking about life on the prairie. Leona knew it could be harsh, especially in the winter months. She greatly admired the snow shoes which Antoine had made. He explained that they used them to track prairie bush rabbits and other game to help supplement their winter diet. Spring and summer were, of course, easier seasons in this northern plain, just as it was in North Dakota for the Brys'. Leona learned that Odilon and Antoine spent time fishing and then drying their catch so it could be eaten in winter when game was scarce. Deer, elk, and antelope were hunted in season. One meal that was made while Leona and John visited included the bannock John had spoken of and a rabbit stew which was delicious.

"Antoine, you are a very good cook," remarked Leona.

"Yes, Odilon and I get along pretty well. We take turns cooking when we aren't busy in the fields planting or harvesting or when Odilon is off with some work in Qu'Appelle.

"What kind of work do you do?" asked the curious newcomer in their midst.

Odilon explained that he took odd jobs in town—everything from freighting materials to working in the general store hauling and stocking. In this way they could get through the long winters and buy the items they could not hunt, dry, or catch.

Before John and Leona knew it, the truly wonderful visit came to an end and it was time to board the train to Shaunavon. Odilon and John loaded the luggage back into their wagon and goodbyes were expressed. Leona felt moved to hug the gentle father of her new husband and Odilon as well. Afterwards, she wondered at the emotions present in her being that allowed her to be more forward than was her nature. "Perhaps," Leona mused, "the sharing of pain as well as joy opens us up to a closeness we would not have had." After a quick stop at the post office where Leona could mail the letters she had written, they were on their way.

Leona and John had discussed the fact that their trip would take about 10 hours to reach Shaunavon. Again, they were blessed with enough food packed in their basket to eat throughout the trip. This time Leona happily observed that Antoine and John had packed dried meat, bannock bread, and fresh berries as well as some of the leftover stew which they would eat first while it was fresh. In addition, her thoughtful father-in-law included some extra fruit, potatoes, and dried meat so a meal or two could be prepared when they arrived in Shaunavon.

"So John, now that I know about Qu'Appelle, what can you tell me about this new town in which we will be living?" asked Leona.

"The town at this point has about 60 businesses which came about after the railroad came to Shaunavon. There is a school, church, and newspaper and it seems to be growing quickly from a village to a town," replied John.

John elected not to fill Leona in at this time about the history of prejudice toward Métis that seemed to come with the settlers in the area.

After a while, John broached a subject which he felt he had ignored for long enough. "I am hoping, Leona, that you will not be too disappointed in my cabin. It is not as big as Odilon and Father's space and it has become run down in the time I have been away. I did as much work on it as I could before I returned to North Dakota. A friend has made sure it did not blow down in the prairie wind, but there will be much to do, I'm afraid, before it will be comfortable."

"John please don't worry overmuch. I am just happy to be with you. Together we will do whatever is necessary to make it our home."

With that, John relaxed and the couple alternately slept, ate, or visited for the remainder of the next stage of their life journey together.

Afterword

This chapter, which included the coming together and marriage of two individuals with such different backgrounds, and the subsequent visit to Antoine and Odilon, has little basis in fact other than the date and location of the marriage and the historical events described by Antoine. However, the depiction of the characters does come from a place deep in my heart. Months and months of study and research has enabled me to envision the dance that occurred as each of the actors in the play became a part of a culture so distinct from one another but were able to find, through love, the common ground between them. As I listened to the voices of my ancestors, I accepted my oneness with each of them.

It is easy to see why Grandma would have felt such a connection with John, a man who came from a culture which cherished strong family kinship ties, something Grandma had never experienced but clearly felt, on some level, a yearning for, an elusive missing piece. Although none of my characterization of John's family is firsthand knowledge, research did show that Antoine and Odilon lived in Qu'Appelle where together they homesteaded. It was after studying the Métis and their values and traditions that I was able to create a believable and close family structure among the Ouellette's. I imagine that were John able to express the love he felt for his mother and if Leona had been able to observe the closeness between John, his father, and his brother as this story depicts, Leona would have gleaned insight into her own life. One expects an individual to then strive to build strong relationships in one's own family and I believe this was a motivational factor for Leona as she began life with John. I have no firsthand knowledge of the feelings John harbored concerning the loss of a way of life and the disappointment at the hands of the government, the educational system and the Euro-American settlers. However, my research on the Métis culture indicates these people had to have felt abandoned.

Again, this portion of the story describes Grandma as an intelligent person whose thoughts often ran to analysis. According to the letters in my possession, she followed the political scene and in one letter to my sister, clearly advocated a choice that she staunchly stood behind. She had discovered that my sister intended to vote for Grandma's choice and the letter thanked her. In it, Grandma was adamant that her candidate had been "vilified, misrepresented, misquoted, spied upon and even lied about." One could feel the emotion in Grandma's words. In another letter, Grandma enumerated the magazines she subscribed to: *Time, U.S. News and World Report, The National Observer*, two religious magazines, one garden magazine and one Senior Citizens magazine as well as various seed catalogues which she said she had enjoyed, "since I was a little girl."

Grandma proclaimed that her education taught her "patriotism and a love of the Lord." This and the view of world events through the eyes of John would have been in conflict. Grandma would have felt a great deal of dissonance upon hearing the treatment of John and the Métis culture by the U.S. government. She would not have been averse to expressing her opinion when the topic was close to her heart.

In the same letter thanking my sister for voting for the right candidate, Grandma shared her belief that, in most cases, the U.S. engaging in war is a dishonorable and unpatriotic thing to do. Grandma describes being "disillusioned." She declares that the only reason to declare war would be if we are attacked. We see a woman who is passionate about what she sees as "right and moral." Clearly the treatment of John's culture would have been immoral in her eyes.

As far as level of schooling, higher education was not available to this intelligent woman and I suspect she carried some measure of regret, Lack of formal schooling did not, however, keep her from expressing definite views. Grandma's comments in the story about women's voting rights would fit into her view of herself and the world. She knew she was every bit as smart as a man and therefore would have been an excellent voter, despite her lack of education.

I am imagining that had Grandma an opportunity to spend time in the home of Antoine and Odilon, to hear the stories associated with their history and to experience the songs of their heart, she could not have helped but be moved as I was when I read articles describing how Métis of current times still hold to the oral traditions which sustain them. That the Métis were given official recognition in 1982 by the Canadian government as an Aboriginal people was a start. And on July 20, 2013 the Bell of Batoche was unveiled and restored to the Métis people of Western Canada at the annual festival, "Back to Batoche." The historic bell is pockmarked in several places with bullets fired by Canadian military forces at the Battle of Batoche in 1885 in which the Métis were fighting for land rights and national recognition. The Canadian army defeated the Métis forces led by Gabriel Dumond and Louis Riel. The bell had been taken from the church in Batoche where it had hung, and was taken back to Ontario as a war trophy. Imagine being one of the 400,000 Métis hearing the sacred bell ring over Batoche for the first time in more than a century! May that reverberation ignite a sense of peace.

I sense my characters speaking to me of their very human desires and needs. On a deep level I feel their suffering and I salute the courage it took for these individuals to step forward and become vulnerable in their quest to find love. Through these connections to our families both in our present lifetimes and well before our births, my hope is that we are led to clearer understandings and discoveries of who we really are and our place in the matrix of life.

John & Leona Ouellette and Wedding Party

Antoine and Odilon Ouellette

John Wells Family

Chapter 4

At last the couple heard the roaring sound of the steam locomotive give way to a lazy yawn, a signal they had reached their final destination. There was the clang of couplings and slowly the metal wheels screeched to a halt. Although train travel was a blessing, Leona was indeed happy to get away from the stifling heat onboard. A cool drink of water was foremost in her mind as well as finally being able to really stretch her cramped legs. None of these complaints did the newly married woman express for it was her goal to look on the bright side, especially during this arrival in Shaunavon. Leona realized that John was uneasy about bringing his wife to his rustic cabin and she wished to calm his fears with an optimistic outlook.

"Well, Leona," John remarked with a grin, "Last chance to decide whether you want to get off here or buy a return ticket."

"Oh John, I am excited to begin our new life. I am not a wallflower so do not worry that I am afraid of hard work. Together we can do whatever is necessary to make your cabin our home."

John smiled at Leona's comments and together they struggled to remove their belongings from the train. John had mentioned that they would be met at the station by a friend and sure enough, there was a gentleman who waved at John and rushed up to help with the luggage.

"Leona, this is Johnny Wells. I'd like you to meet Leona, Johnny."

Johnny gave a shy grin and nodded his head.

"Oh," thought Leona, "another quiet man." Leona saw a resemblance between the two and assumed that Johnny was also a Métis. Like her John, this neighbor had the dark hair, high cheek bones and darker skin that she admired in her husband.

"The wagon is in the back of the station," remarked Johnny as he lifted the trunk as if it weighed very little. The three trudged to their destination where Leona spotted a roomy wagon pulled by a smart looking horse. Immediately John went up to the handsome animal who snorted a "hello."

"Ah, you are glad to see me back, eh Kastitesow?" said John as he caressed the animal.

John addressed Leona to tell her that Johnny had kept Kastitesow during the time John was absent from his cabin.

"I can tell you missed both of these friends, John. Is Kastitesow a Michif word?" asked Leona.

"It is actually a Cree word meaning black. He is such a beautiful ebony color I thought it very appropriate."

With that, the three climbed onto the wagon, John took the reins and they were on their way. Their journey took them into wide open prairie spaces where Leona observed both sod houses and cabins—sometimes fences for chickens, small barns and occasional hay silos. Not far from the dirt road, there appeared to be forested slopes.

"Are those really trees I am seeing?" Leona asked with a feeling of joy.

"Yes, Leona, this area is rich with springs and ponds and forests in the midst of grasslands," answered John. "I wondered if this would please you," remarked John with a gleam in his eyes. "There is no big city as yet like Qu'Appelle but the land is beautiful here."

"Do you live near John's cabin, Johnny?" asked Leona.

"Yes, my place is less than a half mile away so often John and I have been able to rely on each other. It is good to have a neighbor and friend you can depend on," replied Johnny seriously.

"I'm not sure what I would have done without you around to take care of my place when I found it necessary to look for work elsewhere, Johnny. I will always be grateful to you," expressed John just as seriously.

Leona had a notion that these two men rarely discussed their true feelings and she felt honored to be present for these moments.

"I understand that you and John grew up together in Lewistown, Johnny," remarked Leona.

"Yes, Leona. As a matter of fact, for a time we all lived in a large dwelling that held both the Ouellette and the Well's families. I was about 10 years younger than John so I looked up to him. He took me under his wing and taught me much about hunting and fishing and becoming a man. We have had some good times. I was pretty sad when John decided to move up here, but eventually I was able to join him. I have some family members that live close and the land available in Lewistown became scarcer as the big ranchers moved in so it turned out to be a good move for me."

"Are you married, Johnny?" asked Leona hopefully. Having another woman that she could befriend in this new experience might make things easier, thought Leona.

"No," answered Johnny wistfully. "I would like to have a wife but so far I do not."

It was still light out when the three arrived at Johnny's cabin. "You can take the wagon and of course, Kastitesow, and I'll come get it later. Yours is in your shed. I'll stop by tomorrow and see if there is anything I can help you with. As far as I can tell, the cabin is in fine shape as is the chicken coop, fence, and your shed. I know you will be busy preparing the soil for your garden. I am glad you are back, John. Oh, by the way, I brought you some provisions that are in the wagon so you will have food for a few days."

John's reply included a smiling face and sincere thanks for all Johnny had done and then the couple was on their way. Just up the road, in fact, Leona spotted a cabin with a wooden roof and shingles. There were two windows facing the front as well. Johnny's cabin was a similar design and Leona suspected that John had assisted Johnny in building his when he had arrived in this area. "How glad I am that John has a friend to depend on and that we have a neighbor so close," thought Leona.

John drove around back of the cabin, climbed down from the wagon and opened the door of a small barn with two stalls, a wagon, tools and a stack of firewood. "I see that Johnny has refreshed my wood supply and put fresh hay and feed in Kastitesow's stall." John unhitched the horse from the wagon, spoke to Kastitesow in his calm and gentle way as he led him into his stall and then proceeded to unload the wagon. John knew he would be back soon to brush his fine four-footed friend. Anxious to get inside and see her new home, Leona helped carry the bags and soon John had opened the back door to the cabin.

Leona stood in the doorway and weighed her impressions. John watched to see Leona's reaction to what she saw. Nervous about her feelings, John waited patiently while she examined the interior. A wood stove stood in the corner not unlike the one she had used in North Dakota. Beside it was a small stack of firewood. On the other side of the room was a table with two chairs, two stools, and shelves holding dishes, kerosene lamps, a coffee pot and several cast iron frying pans, as well as several of the birch bark baskets John had mentioned that his mother created. In the corner she spotted a fine-looking butter churn. Further into the cabin Leona saw two wooden rocking chairs as well as a bed. A wooden chest sat at the foot of the bed. On the floor were handsome hooked rugs with colorful flower designs surrounded by leaves and tendrils that Leona suspected had been made by John's mother, Angelique. Earlier John had explained that these were made from old clothing that his mother had cut into strips.

With a twinkle in her eyes, Leona declared, "Why John, this looks very cozy!"

Leona was secretly smiling to herself with the thought that John had probably pulled out some of his mother's homemade items to "pretty up" the interior when he was here last. How grateful she felt for his thoughtfulness.

"With some sweeping and scrubbing and a few of the niceties I have in my chest, I imagine we will be quite comfortable," remarked Leona with a smile at her new husband. "I love the touches from your mother, too."

John's entire body relaxed before Leona's eyes.

"I know, Leona, there is much work to do but we will do it together."

John went to the barn to properly brush and feed Kastitesow and then returned to the cabin to help Leona unpack their belongings. Afterwards he took Leona outside to show her the area where they would soon begin planting their garden. Sturdy branches had been tied to horizontal split logs which were placed tightly together to form a fence around the soon to be garden. Leona knew this would keep rabbits and other animals from helping themselves to the crops. Beside it was another small fenced-in area where chickens would be placed as soon as John could acquire some. A small chicken coop was visible as well as the outhouse.

Thanks to the nest egg given them by Lewis, John would buy a cow so there would be milk and butter. Next to the house, John pointed out an underground cellar he had dug to store food. All in all, Leona was very pleased with what she saw and complimented John on his structures.

In addition, John took Leona down to the stream where fresh water could be obtained and showed her the buckets and small cart available to transport the water. Fortunately, the water source was close so their personal needs, as well as water for the garden, would be available. Leona realized that having a well, as her father had in North Dakota, was a luxury.

It dawned on Leona that she would have much to learn about operating a farm in this new land. Although used to helping in her father's homestead in North Dakota, Leona suspected her jobs here would be many. Thankfully Leona was strong and determined in this regard, and knew she was capable of this challenge. She, in fact, welcomed it. The list making began immediately!

The first thing on Leona's list was to get the stove working so the couple could heat water and cook a simple meal before she found herself completely exhausted. Leona realized that the worry and anxiety of the day had taken much of her energy. The meal and getting linens on the bed would be the last tasks of this day.

John had brought in a large bucket of fresh water he had obtained from the stream and assisted in stoking up the stove. In the bag given them by Johnny, Leona found coffee, flour, butter, eggs, sugar, milk, oatmeal, bacon and potatoes. She could see that this would be a feast for the couple. For this meal, potatoes and eggs would be perfect!

Before long, the couple sat down at their little table on which Leona had placed a tablecloth from her chest. The day was beginning to wane, so she had lit a candle and placed it in the center of the table. Across the room, an oil lamp flickered by the bed on which Leona had placed fresh linens and the treasure found in the blanket box at the end of the bed: one of Angelique's beautiful quilts. Bowing their heads and holding hands, Leona thanked God for their safe journey, their satisfying meal, and their new life together.

The next morning, Leona awoke feeling refreshed and ready to take on some tasks around the cabin. She saw that John was already up and noticed that he had lit the stove and brought in a fresh bucket of water so Leona could begin breakfast. Some of the bacon along with a bowl of oatmeal and coffee sounded just right and before long the couple was again sitting at their small table thanking God for their blessings. Leona was happy to notice that John did not resist the prayer and that perhaps he was ready to let go of some of the resentments he had held about his faith, although she chose not to question him about this.

"Leona, my first order of business is to hitch up Katitisaw to the wagon and drive over to Johnny's. I need to go into town and purchase a cow so we can have fresh milk and buy some chickens too. I think Johnny could help me choose well. We will keep our cow in his pasture for the time being. Is there anything you need me to get for you?"

"That sounds like a fine idea, John. I can't think of anything I need right now. I plan to make myself more familiar with my surroundings and do some household chores. After that I'd like to begin preparing the ground for a garden. Another job will be to begin sewing curtains for our windows. I am grateful that I have some fabric in my chest thanks to my mother's forward thinking."

"The list is long, isn't it Leona? We will be very busy getting all the chores done in order to be ready for the winter months. I will be happy to have you working beside me." John expressed this with his eyes twinkling and Leona again felt grateful she had made the decision to be John's wife.

After John left, Leona began digging in her trunk to find the seeds she had carefully placed in a box so she could begin planning the garden. Leona had been sending for seed catalogues for several years and she and

Zada, also a gardener, had pored over them. In addition, the Farmer's Almanac gave the ladies information on when was the best time to plant certain crops. Leona had made charts to organize the plantings. According to John, the weather was more temperate here than it was in her home in North Dakota with less snowfall in the winter months. Leona thought that a very nice change.

After changing into an old housedress and apron, Leona felt ready to begin. She found the tools John had mentioned leaving for her in the back and was anxious to examine the soil. She hoped to find it rich enough to produce abundantly. Pleased that this looked to be so, Leona began breaking up the ground with the tools on hand, removing large rocks and raking it smoothly. Leona could tell that it had not been too many seasons since John had planted crops even though she still wished she had manure or fish to use to amend the soil. "Perhaps after we obtain our chickens we will be able to add nutrients to our soil," thought Leona.

Upon examining her charts, Leona realized that this being early May she could begin safely planting brussels sprouts, cauliflower, lettuce, onions, radishes, spinach, swiss chard, turnips and potatoes. Later in the month she would add broccoli, cabbage, carrots, kale, leeks and peas. Leona was so grateful that a fence had already been built around the garden to protect her treasured vegetables.

Leona had in mind to build herself a window box in which she would grow hyssop which was useful as a digestive aid and for colds, and lavender which was helpful for insomnia, nervousness and pain. She also wanted to grow marjoram, savory and thyme for her cooking. Although all the plans were exhausting to think about, Leona was excited as well. After all, this was to be her first home with her new husband and she wanted so to prove to be a good wife and homemaker.

The hours flew by as Leona worked to prepare her garden and she realized it was time to prepare supper. She expected that soon John would return from his errands and would have an appetite. Leona planned to cook extra because she guessed Johnny would be accompanying John in order to bring back whatever livestock John purchased. Leona got busy lighting the stove and preparing biscuits. She was delighted to remember she had packed some jars of homemade jam in her trunk that would be a welcome treat. Bacon and potatoes as well as fruit from Antoine would accompany the meal.

While her oven and stove were busy, Leona took time to wash up, comb her hair, and put on a clean dress and apron. Setting the table came next. Wishing she had some fresh flowers, Leona vowed to pick some prairie wild flowers she had spotted while working on the soon-to-be garden, if there was time before supper.

As it turned out, Leona was picking wild flowers when she heard the wagons drive up, one being driven by John and pulled by Katitesow. Johnny and his horse and wagon followed. In John's wagon Leona noticed hay, oats, and chicken feed. Tied to John's wagon was a lovely brown cow. In John's wagon Leona spotted several chickens in wire cages.

"Oh good," thought Leona, "fresh eggs and milk." She was glad she had some experience milking the cows on her father's farm so she could help John with that chore. Leona knew that Johnny's pasture was near and convenient for her to access each morning, but she suspected that right now the cow might need to be milked.

John stopped the wagon, unhitched Katitesow, and led him into the small barn where he could be fed and brushed. He led the cow in as well to the second stall.

"Does our beauty need to be milked?" asked Leona.

"Yes, I think we are about to get our first pail of fresh milk! Would you like to take care of her while I brush Katitesow?"

"Indeed I would," replied Leona quickly. With that she ran back to the house to fetch a shiny bucket she had carefully sterilized earlier by pouring boiling water into it.

"John, if you have no objections, I would like to name our new acquisition Beauty. She certainly is a fine animal!"

"That sounds just fine," replied John with a twinkle in his eyes.

"All right Beauty, it is time for us to get acquainted. I am Leona and very happy to have you join our family." With that Leona pulled up the stool and placed the bucket carefully under Beauty. Remembering that some cows tended to kick, Leona began using a gentle rhythm to coax the milk from the teats. First leaning her head into the cow's side and talking softly to Beauty, Leona took hold firmly to let the cow know who was in charge and then began squeezing and stroking. The sound of streams of milk foaming into the bucket was such a welcome sound.

During the time John was brushing Katitesow and Leona was milking Beauty, Johnny was delivering the chickens to their coop. Over the course of a day the little farm had become a busy enterprise. When the three farmers were through with their chores, Leona invited the men into the house for their meal.

After washing up, they all sat down to the delicious looking biscuits and potatoes with healthy chunks of bacon. Again, Leona led a prayer of thanks for the gift of the day filled with abundance. The conversation around the table that night allowed Leona to become more familiar with her new neighbor and to see that the men valued their friendship with one another. John complimented Leona on what she accomplished in the garden and Johnny thanked her for allowing him to join their meal.

"Leona, Johnny has generously gifted us a piglet as soon as his mother sow gives birth. It will be a fine thing to have our own source of meat."

"Oh thank you Johnny. Please know that you are always welcome at this table for some home-cooking and conversation. I only hope I can meet a fellow woman with whom I can have such a close relationship as you and John have. I do miss my good friend, Zada from back home."

The evening passed quickly with dishes to be done and time before sundown to begin work on Leona's sewing project. Two tired but contented individuals made ready for bed early with their minds busy on the next day's chores.

Each day brought mild weather and as May and June passed Leona's crops began to grow into beautiful vegetables. The Ouellette's were able to thin the carrots and lettuce and have fresh salads with their meals. John had made Leona a planter box in which she planted the herbs to add to her dishes and also to hang to dry for future use.

Leona had explored the areas around the little cabin and was anxiously awaiting the ripening of Saskatoon berries as well as blueberries and lingonberries. She could almost taste the pies and jams she was aching to make. In addition, Leona planned to pick and dry as many berries as possible for the coming winter. These would add important nutrition to many dishes. John had taught Leona the method of mashing the Saskatoons and then drying them into cakes. In that way pieces could be broken off in the winter and boiled or added to soups and stews. In fact, Leona was anxious to make the nutritious pemmican which John and Johnny both remembered from their youth and into which she would add berries.

The two men had spent many a day hunting and had come home with wild turkeys and deer. The traps they set out netted gophers, rabbits and prairie chickens. In addition, the fishing in the river behind the cabins brought fresh trout to add to the storehouse. Some of the fresh meat and fish fed the family and much of it was dried by the men to save for the winter months. Leona and John were feeling very prosperous and Johnny's presence was part of that satisfaction.

Leona had continued in the same vein her mother had modeled for her concerning the schedule for a prairie wife's duties. Monday was washday. This involved building a roaring fire out back and hanging a vat of water over the flames until boiling. After boiling, the clothes and linens were lifted out of the vat by a paddle and scrubbed on a washboard with lye soap, then put in a second tub for rinsing. A line was hung outside for drying. Wanting so to be a mother, Leona often wondered at the extra efforts involved with adding children's soiled clothes to this already burdensome task!

Tuesday was ironing day. Leona would heat the iron on the stove which would need to continue blazing until this chore was completed. On warm days, the extra heat and smoke in the kitchen led Leona to decide that some items could just go without ironing!

Saturday evening was bath time. The couple preferred, on warm days, to bathe in the creek out back, but when the weather did not cooperate, water would need to be boiled on the stove and poured into a washtub set up on the kitchen floor.

Cooking, sewing, gardening, cleaning, taking care of the chickens and Beauty—Leona found herself very busy indeed. Some nights she would literally fall into bed and wonder where the day had gone. What Leona really missed were the hours she used to be able to lose herself in a good book. Although she had tucked some into her chest, there just had been no time of late for this relaxation. Come winter, Leona promised herself, she would be sure to make room in her schedule for reading and letter writing. She was anxious to reconnect with her father and Zada as soon as possible.

Marriage, Leona was finding, could be a lonely experience. John was often with Johnny, hunting or fishing or taking care of the other chores involved with prairie life. On occasion, Leona would express an interest in accompanying John into the small town when he went to the mercantile or feed store. Whenever the question came up, Leona noticed a cloud pass over John's features and he would immediately respond in a gruff way with some excuse or other. Leona's feelings were hurt at these times but she chose not to make an issue of it.

Not given to dwelling on problems, Leona continued with the hard work of living on the prairie and found the summer slipping away. September already and she could feel the change in the air. The temperature was dropping but still was comfortable for all the outdoor work necessary to harvest, store and dry crops. Inside, Leona was occupied canning and storing foods in preparation for the winter months.

As busy as she was Leona was shocked when she realized, "I believe I am with child!" As much as she wanted a child Leona wondered what John's reaction would be. The wall John had thrown up made Leona afraid to share this wonderful coming event with her husband. This hesitation, however, did not last long because Leona's practical side realized this was obviously not something she could keep a secret. "Nor should I!" declared Leona with her natural strength and stubbornness winning out.

When John came into the cabin later, Leona had taken pains to tidy up around the house, plan a nice meal and put on a clean dress. No matter John's reaction, this announcement deserved special attention and Leona would give it its due. As luck would have it, John seemed to be in a good mood and began telling Leona about his success fixing the wagon wheel that had broken and helping Johnny repair part of the pasture fence.

"I also have some good news, John," began Leona. "Today I dug around in my trunk and found my knitting needles and some yarn I had tucked away inside it. I plan to knit a small sweater for a visitor soon to arrive to the Ouellette household."

These words were expressed with sparkling eyes and John's response could not have been more welcome.

"We are going to have a baby?" John asked with a quivering voice.

Nodding her assent, Leona asked John how he felt about a baby joining them. John demonstrated his elation by grabbing Leona and swinging her around the small space in their cabin laughing in such a hearty way. Leona was very pleased.

"I was worried that perhaps you would not think it such happy news," admitted Leona.

"I do not understand why you would be worried about this, Leona," John declared.

"Lately, John I have wondered if you were ashamed of me or tiring of my company. When I have asked to accompany you to town your response has left me baffled."

"Oh Leona, how sorry I am that your feelings have been hurt. I will attempt to explain. I see that I should have voiced my fears long ago and included you in my thinking. I have been trying to protect you, and I see that has not been fair to you. You have not, as yet, experienced the prejudice and shunning that Johnny and I and other Métis grew up with. We are used to other settlers in the community not accepting us or our ways. I cannot bear the idea of you being exposed to hateful comments or looks just because you have chosen to marry a mixed blood."

Leona's first reaction was anger. Not anger directed at John, but at those who would so judge another based on such superficial reasoning. But with as much self-control as she could muster, Leona responded to John's words.

"Oh John! I should have figured this out on my own. It is unlike me to jump to conclusions and to allow my emotions to run rampant. You explained to me when I first met you what it was like to grow up in an environment of intolerance. I should have realized this is a predicament you would find anywhere there are settlers who are not Métis. My only excuse is I expect my pregnancy has contributed to these runaway feelings. We will stand together in this!"

With that the couple came together with tears in their eyes. Leona, saddened by John's words but relieved that his love for her was still present. John, feeling guilty for not being honest and vowing to do better. Both of them, happy about the news of a new addition to their lives.

Afterword

This chapter felt so close to my heart as I imagined these two young lovers settling into their sweet cabin in Saskatchewan and beginning to build their new life together. I anticipated the possible struggles and suffering that was apt to be their experience as well. In order to write a valid account of this life, I acquainted myself with the hardships of prairie life in this timeframe and the homesteaders who settled in this area in my research. Studying the Métis, I learned of the traditional foods that were an important part of their culture and specifically in the area of Shaunavon, the types of game available to the hunters. In addition, I realized that the Métis connection to the Catholic Church, as well as their close kinship ties, were an integral part of their identities. These proud people, for whom traditions and family meant so much, faced challenges that often stripped them of these identities and left them longing for their pasts.

In bringing these two personalities together, I took into account John's family history as well as Leona's largely unknown background having been raised by people other than her birth family. My memories of Grandma support what my research tells me of the German personality. Although raised by two individuals of Irish background, Grandma seemed to me to be of stoic German stock. The stereotypes following this race of hardworking, efficient and disciplined traits fit her perfectly. Leona's hard work in Shaunavon expressed this tendency to put her nose to the grindstone and accomplish what needed to be done. Grandma was a practical thinker, never silly, but when she smiled one knew it was genuine. In addition, Grandma was a planner and an organizer. In my possession is a planting diary that Grandma kept religiously, enumerating when certain plants were put in the ground, which lived, which flourished and the best locations for certain of these. I suspect Grandma began such an organized way of life in her first home in Shaunavon. The shadow side of these traits can mean that when a person is not able, for one reason or another, to plan and organize, unable to control a situation, there is accompanying stress and anguish. Grandma suffered from these feelings.

Another German personality tendency is the belief that traditions are important. That John and Leona had a common background in Catholicism probably contributed to Leona's comfort. Grandma left her Catholic roots at some point in her later adult life and became part of another church. This must have been a hard-fought decision. Grandma was angry with the Catholic Church over a personal issue and left it, not unlike John when his people were treated so harshly in the mission school. However, later in her life, she came back to the religion of her birth and childhood, back to the tradition that was so important to her.

As the reader can see, I have begun to paint John with the brush of fear and helplessness. These feelings were understandably brought on by his history as a Métis in a country that did not accept his culture. The unfortunate result was John's inability to discuss these worries with Leona.

Here is the beginning of a crumbling foundation that, as you will see, even Leona's stubborn tendencies may not be able to repair.

Métis Basket

Métis Beadwork

Flag of the Métis People

Chapter 5

Leona continued to think about this new child the two of them were bringing into the world and began to ask herself some important questions. If John was afraid to expose Leona to the townsfolk, what would it be like to raise a child here? Was John really protecting Leona or himself from more of the derision he had experienced in the past? Was Leona being naïve to imagine that a different result might be possible? These questions filled Leona's mind, until she knew a conversation had to take place soon.

The summer proved to be an especially busy time for the household. Leona looked over the garden and sewed baby clothes for the new addition, as well as her daily chores. John and Johnny continued to hunt game and plan for the winter months. With the fall came harvesting chores. Leona was actively canning vegetables and drying fruits for the same purpose. She was very happy to see the shelves that John had added to the kitchen filling up with these goods. However, in the back of her mind, there lingered the same questions she had been asking at the beginning of the summer.

One pleasant fall afternoon when John was taking a much-needed break from his chores around the property, Leona asked John to chat with her for a few moments. Some just baked cookies and tea were placed on their cozy kitchen table and Leona began to speak.

"John, I have been yearning to have a heart to heart with you ever since our conversation the day I told you we were going to have a child. Do you remember our discussion?"

John had a very good idea what the content of Leona's chat might be and knowing Leona as he now did after several months of marriage, he had not expected her to let go of her desires to go to town. "She's right. This must be discussed," thought John to himself.

"Yes, Leona, I remember well how upset you were that I avoided allowing you to accompany me to town."

"Well, John, then you are probably aware of my request. I have some things I will need at the mercantile store that involve sewing projects for the baby and other items for after she or he is born. These are not the kind of items a man, even as able as you, could select, and I believe it is high time we quit hiding in our little cabin."

John loved the part of Leona that was direct and no nonsense, but, in this instance, he was ill at ease with the idea of this trip to town together. In spite of his feelings, he knew it was time for this next step in their lives.

"Just let me know when you would like to go, and I will plan that trip with you."

Leona loved this husband of hers so much at this moment, that she nearly knocked her tea over grabbing his sweet face and kissing him.

"Thank you, John. Let's go tomorrow afternoon after all the chores are done. It won't take me long to pick out what I need, and we'll be home in time to get supper started!"

The next afternoon, true to his word, John brought the wagon around, helped Leona climb up beside him, and they were off on the relatively short trip to town. John shared with Leona that the railroad had purchased land and it would go up for sale soon. The natural result would mean more settlers moving in, and although John foresaw the building of more businesses to serve the people, he feared what more white settlers would mean to the Métis in the community.

"When we first moved here, Johnny mentioned that some of his relatives live in the area. You said there is a community of Métis here in Shaunavon. Isn't it about time I met some of them?" asked Leona firmly.

John answered in the affirmative. "Yes, Leona. As a matter of fact, Johnny and I had discussed the fact that we've been so busy we haven't been in touch with any of our people. I told him I was hopeful you would be interested in meeting some of them."

"Well, you silly! Of course I would love to meet folks. I have felt a little lonely spending so much time by myself and visiting would suit me to a tea!"

As they approached the small town, Leona felt encouraged that at last she might begin to feel as if she belonged in this new country. John helped Leona down, tied up the wagon and accompanied her past the feed store, the small chapel, and on to the mercantile. Leona wished there was a permanent priest stationed in town as she had missed her regular Sunday church services, but she was hopeful that the new influx of people would be able to support such a venture.

The store was small, but Leona found the sewing items she needed and moved on to some more personal items. John was her silent companion, and before long the couple was ready to pay for their purchases. Although feeling nervous herself, Leona felt a need to introduce herself to the owner of the shop.

"Hello, I am Mrs. Ouellette, new to the area. Your shop is very nice."

There was silence from the gentleman behind the counter, but finally he looked up and said, "Will that be all?"

Leona was just stubborn enough not to respond to the dismissal, and in her sweetest voice, declared that it was. John paid for the items and the two departed.

"Well, now. That wasn't so bad, was it? A bit rude, but we must hold our heads high and know that we have just as much right as anyone to live in this area and shop in this store!" declared Leona with a gleam in her eyes.

John was again so grateful for this strong wife of his, who was not about to kowtow to anyone. The ride home was much more relaxing, and soon the two were planning an event with the other Métis in the area.

The next day, Johnny came over and the three decided that while the weather was still reasonably warm, it would be a good time to plan a get together. Johnny declared that he would like to use his yard as the gathering place. He had been making some benches for just such a purpose and had an area that would serve for music and dancing. Leona would provide several main dishes for the event and Johnny said that everyone would contribute to the potluck. The boys would take care of inviting everyone, since Leona had not had the pleasure of meeting any of their friends.

Leona was so looking forward to the party! She had been cooking for several days. Her pork and beans were bubbling on the stove, and she had pies lined up on the counter as well as several loaves of bread. To add to the fare, John had just finished smoking some fish he had caught. The weather was cooperating. Soon the two would load up their goodies and head to Johnny's home a bit before the others so Leona could set out the foodstuffs.

Johnny greeted the Ouellettes with a big smile as they drove up and predicted that everyone who had been invited would show up. After all, they were anxious to meet John's wife! These words made Leona cringe, and as she peeked out from her bonnet, Johnny's grin was apparent.

"I am sorry, Leona, to have obviously made you uncomfortable. Do not worry. Everyone will love you as do John and I."

Leona had been in Johnny's cabin before, and so made a beeline with her hot items to heat on the stove, while the boys saw to the horse and wagon. As she looked out Johnny's kitchen window, she spotted the fine-looking benches he had placed around the yard and the raked area where she suspected the dancing would take place. In addition, a long wide board had been laid on several saw horses where Leona knew the offerings of food would find a home. Luckily, Leona had brought along some tablecloths and flowers to fancy up the picnic. John had mentioned that each family would bring their own plate, cup and utensils, as well as a dish to share. Large pitchers of iced tea, which Johnny had prepared, graced each end of the table as well.

Before long, John and Johnny joined Leona in the yard, and they heard the sounds of buggies and horses stopping out front. Johnny ran around to guide each family to the spot where they could graze their horses. People began to file into the yard where the couple sat. John grabbed

Leona's hand and gave her a reassuring smile, knowing that his wife's nerves were on edge.

So often what we worry about never comes to pass, and this was Leona's experience on this fine fall afternoon. Each of the visitors shook Leona's hand and greeted her in the Métis way as John had described.

"Tawnshi," (hello) or "Tawnshi kiyawow," (How are you?) were the refrains.

The introductions were made and Leona was graciously welcomed to the community. Leona felt only acceptance and began to quickly relax and enjoy the conversations. She realized that the Métis population was larger than she had known—some of the folks were relatives of Johnny and John and others, Métis who had traveled here more recently.

The table was loaded with delicious choices: cakes made from dried berries, sweet butter to slather on bannock or fried bread, meat pie (or as John taught Leona, La Tourtiere), jerky made from deer, meatballs, steamed pudding, custard . . . so many tasty dishes. The children present ate and then began laughing and playing chase games. Leona was so happy to know she would also soon have a little one to spark up the days.

Many individuals came up to Leona and chatted with her and were so happy to hear of the news of a child due in the spring. In fact, one of the women who had introduced herself as Evelina, and whose family John later told Leona had also made their homes in Lewistown when she was a child, presented Leona with a gift.

"Leona, this is a dream catcher made to protect your sleeping child from nightmares. This little gift will bless your child and any others you may have," affirmed this lovely Métis woman.

"Oh Evelina what a beautiful and thoughtful gift!" exclaimed Leona while a smiling John stood by her side.

Leona and John examined the workmanship and saw that the shape was made of bent wood which formed a round frame. Inside the frame was a web shape.

"Leona, the women tie animal sinew strands to make this strong web," remarked John.

"Look at the beautiful feathers hanging from the frame. Thank you again, Evelina. We will treasure this always," expressed Leona with tears in her eyes.

Before long, the men were picking up their fiddles, harmonicas, and drums and the music began. Nearly instantaneously, the children gathered and began dancing as did their parents. Not since the days Leona had spent with John's father and brother did she feel so relaxed and at peace. The feeling of community, the joy of being together, the lively music, to say nothing of the wonderful food—Leona felt full indeed in both body and soul.

At the end of the day, as the sun began to go down and everyone was full and happy, the company began to leave. Leona felt much loved, as each adult wished her a good evening with the Métis "Bon swear," took her hands and wished her well. Some even hugged this newcomer to let her know she was a welcome addition to the community.

After helping Johnny set things right in his backyard and in his kitchen, the couple said goodbye to their host, climbed up in their wagon and let Kastitesow take them home. John looked at Leona with that gleam in his eyes his wife was coming to know so well and asked her how she felt the day had gone.

"You know as well as I do that this was a very special event for me and that I am so happy you and Johnny planned it. Your friends and family made me feel so welcome. I had worried so that people would not like me or would treat me differently because I am not Métis, but I felt only acceptance this day. I know this is a tribute to you, John, for your people respect you and your choices. Thank you for making this day one I will remember always."

John hugged Leona as they made their way back to their home.

John took Leona to town several times over the course of the fall months before the cold weather and snow set in. When the pair walked along the streets or entered any store in the little town, and no matter whether townspeople turned away as the couple approached, or overtly glared, the message was the same: "You are not our folk."

Leona pondered this often and wondered if these white settlers were afraid of John, and by association, Leona. At the root of so much prejudice, Leona believed lay an underlying fear. She, however, continued to smile and act as if the reception from others was normal. In no way would she give these people the satisfaction of knowing she was really quite hurt, not so much for herself but for John. In addition, Leona worried about bringing a child into this environment and wondered what kind of bigotry their child might experience. Leona did not express these reflections to John for fear of bringing an already hurtful experience to the forefront of his mind, although Leona had reason to believe that John's thoughts were not far from hers on this painful issue. After all, he had had a lifetime of dealing with the judgments of others.

As the winter months arrived, the temperature dropped and the hours of daylight grew shorter. Leona kept busy sewing for the baby and cooking, using the store-house of vegetables and meats the couple had prepared for this time of year. The hardest task by far for Leona, particularly as the baby grew, was the weekly clothes washing. Winter brought more challenges than before. Fortunately, John was good about helping with all of these tasks.

When winter came, the vat for washing clothes was brought inside. It was filled with water and then boiled on the stove and then dumped into a large washtub when heated. This required dozens of pails of water to fill the large tub and a fair amount of wood or cobs. The stove took an hour to heat. Leona would put a pot of navy beans on to simmer slowly, while waiting for the stove to reach a high enough temperature. Once the clothes were scrubbed with the washboard, John would place a tub of water on the back porch for rinsing. Wet items were hung outside on the clothesline. In winter, the frozen clothes would eventually be brought in to hang on backs of chairs around the stove. Leona would later use an iron, which was heated on the stove. All of this was backbreaking work, especially for someone in Leona's condition.

Leona had been writing back home, both to Zada and her father, and had received letters from both. Zada shared that she and Thomas were also expecting their first child. Leona felt homesick, and so longed to see her father, of course, but most especially she longed to visit someone her own age, and her best friend, at that. Now the two had even more in common. By the time the end of March rolled around, Leona and John had begun preparing their garden for planting, and Leona began planting something else in her fertile mind. "Perhaps John would let me ride the train home for a visit."

The more she thought about this, the more Leona was sure John would agree. When she broached the issue, however, John's reaction was unexpected. "But why would you want to leave just now?" The look on John's face expressed so much more than his words. Fear loomed on the face of the man Leona loved so dearly.

As Leona began explaining her thinking, she also assured John that this would be a mere visit and she would return to their happy home. John's body began to relax somewhat, but Leona realized just how deeply John's insecurity lay. The fare for the train was another possible problem, but the pair discussed this and Leona mentioned that her father had offered to send her money for the tickets anytime she wished to visit.

"Leona, I must stay here for as long as possible. This is the season when hunting and gathering must occur so we have food and heat for next winter. Our garden needs to be tended as well. I do not want you to make this long trip by yourself, but how would we do this?"

"John, the baby is not due until the end of May. What if you accompanied me there a week or two before the date? I have also been longing to birth our child there, where I know of a midwife in town. In addition, I would have Zada to help me. I have to admit to being nervous about our first. I want you there, too, of course. We would come back home as soon as I could travel."

This long speech, which Leona had planned carefully beforehand, took much courage, and she felt quite drained afterward waiting for John's answer. In John's slow, cautious way, he looked at Leona, reaching out his hand toward hers and nodded.

"Leona, I have put you through many changes and much hard work. You ask for little and I wish to please you. If this is your desire, let it be so. I think our good friend Johnny would watch over the house and garden while we are gone. When would you like to leave?"

Relieved to tears, Leona responded with a smile and a hug, and the couple discussed the details of the trip. The next day a telegraph was sent to York where Zada and her father lived, and Leona began readying for their trip.

When the day arrived for their departure, Leona was nearly exhausted. She was determined to have the house clean and ready when they brought their new baby home. Everything was washed and ironed and the baby's crib was ready with a blanket lovingly quilted by Leona. She had packed a few clothes for herself and John, some baby clothes for the newborn, and a quilt made for Zada and Thomas' new arrival. In addition, Leona carried a basket with food and drink to last them the long 19 hours of travel they would have before reaching York. Fortunately, her father had sent enough money to buy tickets for open section accommodations, in which the pair of seats could be converted into berths, so John and Leona could sleep for part of the journey.

"I imagine I will sleep much of the way there," thought this tired mother-to-be.

John hauled the belongings out to the wagon, hitched up Kastitesow, and helped Leona up into the seat beside him. Leona had been very grateful for John's attitude since the decisions had been made. He was loving and kind and clearly did want Leona to be happy. There was a quick stop at Johnny's, who would join them and then bring Kastitesow and the wagon back to his cabin to oversee, while the Ouellettes were out of town. Then they were on their way to the train bound for York, North Dakota.

The journey was tiring but catnaps in their berths revived them. At long last their train pulled into the station at York. Not certain her father would be there to meet them yet, Leona scanned the small depot. Happily, she caught a glimpse of her father as he drove up in his wagon. When Lewis spotted Leona and John, the grin on his face mirrored Leona's.

Lewis hurried over to meet the couple and gently gave Leona a hug.

"Let me look at you, Leona. You look healthy and well, and for that I am grateful. I have missed you, Leona. I'm so glad you decided to make this trip. Thank you, John for accompanying my daughter," remarked Lewis as he shook John's hand.

"My thanks to you, sir, for sending us the money for the train tickets. Leona really wanted to have our baby here, and I would not miss the birth for anything."

After retrieving the suitcases, the men shepherded Leona to the wagon and helped her aboard. The trip to her father's house was short. Soon the three were sitting around Lewis' kitchen table drinking coffee and eating toast spread with blueberry jam. Lewis filled his daughter and son-in-law in on the local news, and Leona asked after her friend, Zada, and her husband, Thomas. When told that Zada had invited the party to her home for supper that evening, Leona was delighted.

With that, John's weary wife yawned, and her thoughtful husband suggested she nap for a few hours. Suddenly feeling so tired, Leona agreed and was soon sound asleep in the spare bedroom.

By the time Leona woke up, much of the afternoon had slipped by, and she knew it was time to get ready for their supper engagement. Wandering into her father's kitchen, she spotted some leftover lunch which she had clearly slept through. Nibbling on some cheese and bread, as well as a piece of fruit, Leona returned to the bedroom to unpack, freshen up, and change into a clean dress.

"Hello sleepyhead!" teased John, as he joined Leona in the bedroom. "I see you have finally finished your slumber. It is good for both you and the baby to have rested today." John proceeded to tell Leona that after lunch, Lewis had taken John through the town to show him the new mercantile shop and to stop by the livery where Lewis worked.

After hearing of their trip into town, Leona wondered if John had felt any of the prejudice the two of them experienced in Shaunavon. "Perhaps it is a different situation when two men are walking together, one of them clearly of Indian or Métis heritage, than it is when one of the couple is a white woman." Before her experience in Shaunavon, Leona would never have considered the possibility of this scenario. "I surely have been very naïve," thought Leona sadly.

Once the three of them had cleaned up, they boarded the wagon and set off for Zada and Thomas' home. Leona had picked a lovely bouquet of wild flowers from her father's backyard and tied them with a yellow ribbon to give to Zada. John could see that Leona was very excited to be reunited with her best friend, and he knew the girls would have much to catch up on.

As the visitors pulled up to Zada's house, Leona could see how lovingly they had planted flowers in the front yard and built a small fence around it. Bird houses, probably constructed by Thomas, hung from the branches of a large fir tree, with lovely meadowlarks flitting back and forth. Anxious to hug her friend, Leona impatiently waited for John to help her down from the wagon. In the meantime, Zada had spotted the wagon and was dashing from the house to meet her guests.

Words were unnecessary, as the two dear friends hugged each other. Tears rolled down each of their bright faces and they laughed at themselves and their wild emotions. The men shook hands with Thomas and the group headed for the house, as the ladies began chatting as if no time at all had passed since their last visit.

A wonderful supper was served, and everyone remarked about Zada's cooking skills: roast pork, baked potatoes, chilled homemade applesauce, green beans canned from last year's garden and Zada's flakey biscuits smothered in butter. Leona ate as much as she was able but of late had found little room in her stomach. She wondered if this baby was intent on showing itself to the world soon. Zada, too, had remarked that Leona looked very ripe indeed!

With promises to get together the next afternoon, a tired Leona joined her husband and father for their return to Lewis' house. Once in the bedroom and in her night clothes, Leona's head barely hit the pillow before she was out. She was so fortunate to still be able to sleep deeply at this point in her pregnancy. John, tired as well, joined the sleeping Leona.

The next afternoon, John dropped Leona off at Zada's, as was planned, and the two girls continued their conversation from the day before. It felt so wonderful to have another woman to share experiences and feelings concerning Leona's married life with John in Saskatchewan. This connection had been Leona's fondest desire for a long time, and she was greedy to cover every subject possible! It was as if she had suddenly removed the lid from a bottle, and her thoughts were spewing out. Zada was amazed to hear her oftentimes quiet, thoughtful friend, literally bubbling with conversation.

Zada was able to get in a word or two edgewise and so Leona learned that her friend's baby was due towards the end of July. She had been regularly seen by the mid-wife in town and urged Leona to see her as soon as possible. Fortunately, Thomas had a telephone installed recently, so the girls phoned the mid-wife, Martha Johnson, and an appointment was set up for the following day.

The next afternoon, John drove Leona to Mrs. Johnson's home and helped her down from the wagon. "Would you like me to go in with you?" John asked shyly.

"Why, yes, thank you John. I would."

Whether or not this fit into the category of correct propriety, Leona did not care. She was glad John had offered and felt him a welcome support for her just then. The two knocked on the door and were greeted by a smiling middle-aged woman who appeared happy to see the both of them. Ushering John and Leona in, Mrs. Johnson offered them tea and they sat in her kitchen to get acquainted. Mrs. Johnson or Martha, as she requested they call her, set them at ease and made the visit very informal and comfortable. Martha eventually took Leona into a bedroom, where she examined the shy, young almost-mother. The two discussed dates and it was determined that this child would most likely show itself in a week or two. Leona felt excited and apprehensive both, and Martha assured her those were very normal reactions for first time mothers-to-be.

On the way back, Leona shared the information with John, and he held Leona gently and assured her that all would be well. John had such faith in his strong wife, whose stubborn nature would see her through this exciting time.

On Thursday, May 22, 1913, Leona awoke in the wee hours of the morning and knew that the day had come for the birth of their first child. The pains began, and after several hours, there was no doubt in Leona's mind that John needed to hitch up the wagon and bring Martha, the midwife, to her father's home. Leona also requested that John bring Zada, who had promised to be present during Leona's labor. John quickly followed Leona's request and was back in short time with the women. Both John and Lewis felt very relieved that now Leona was in good hands. They retired to the kitchen to have coffee with a nip of whiskey to see them through!

Zada had rushed into Leona's room, and was happy to see that Leona was between pains and able to smile at her friend's arrival. Martha quickly examined Leona and reported that everything was coming along right on schedule. Zada followed Martha's directions and began boiling water and preparing the bed where Leona would deliver the child. The tension in the house was palpable, as John and Lewis drank their spiked coffee in the kitchen and prayed that the baby would be healthy, and that Leona would not have too difficult a time.

By dinnertime, the baby girl decided to make her appearance with a healthy cry heard throughout the house. After cleaning the child and Leona, John was called into the room to see his wife and his new daughter, Edna Frances Ouellette. John observed that Leona looked very tired, but clearly radiant, as she held the bundle in her arms.

"Would you like to hold her John?" asked Leona.

John answered in the affirmative and gently reached down to draw the baby into his arms. Leona felt it a wonderful sight to see this man so lovingly gaze at his first child. The couple had discussed names, just the day before, and decided on Edna, if they were blessed with a girl.

After Martha and Zada returned to their homes, John and Leona cuddled with their new arrival and talked, until Leona's eyes grew heavy and she fell into a deep slumber. John remained in the room, seeing to their new addition, and realized that Edna had been born under the Native American sign of the deer. His grandmother had taught him the animal signs and some of the characteristics that went with each. As he remembered, the deer symbolized the ability to laugh and engage in conversation and have generally a sparkly personality. "Ah," thought John. It will be good to have laughter more often join our home. Hopefully, the shadow side of this sign will be less apparent, and Edna would seldom express the moody, impatient and lazy side. John remembered only too well what that was like as his younger sister, Mary, was also born under this sign. "Oh well, we will love Edna's many faces just as we did Mary!"

By the time Edna was a week old, reluctantly, Leona knew the family must return to their home in Shaunavon. Pushing down the reasons for this reluctance, Leona began planning their departure. John was glad to hear that Leona was ready to make the trip. There were so many chores that needed to be done at home, and he had been feeling anxious. The tickets were purchased, and they were to leave at noon the next day. One more visit with her friend was a must, so John dropped his wife and child off at Zada's the afternoon before they were to leave.

The two women held each other and tears flowed freely.

"I imagine that the fact that I just had a baby is affecting my moods, but I feel as though I may never be able to stop crying," Leona admitted. "I feel such sadness at leaving, and I am unsure of the cause."

"Leona, I have known you for a long time, and we have been closer than most sisters. There is something you are not telling me or you are not admitting to yourself. This should be a happy time. You have a loving husband and a beautiful baby girl, and yet I see such sorrow in you. I know we will miss each other, but there is something else."

An unexpected mood came upon Leona, as she felt a small opening in her heart and a willingness to accept the truth.

"Oh Zada, you do know me so well. It is true that I have been harboring fear at returning to Shaunavon. I know myself to be a strong and often stubborn woman. This has often served me well. I suspect that being a mother is changing me in ways I am not sure I can express. I feel safe and cocooned here—loved by my father, your family, and known by many in the town. I've lived here all my life and it is home. My father is so well respected. Although John is different, for the most part, he has been accepted here, and perhaps I am naïve to believe this, but given time, I think our marriage would flourish. In Shaunavon, our lives are very different. Shaunavon has a history of prejudice from the settlers. I mentioned to you before how we are treated in town. I worry for the sake of my child and any other children we may have. Will they be exposed to the discrimination, and how will it affect them?"

Zada's only answer was to hug her friend and tell her to trust herself and John and to ask God to look after their family.

Nodding in agreement, Leona felt better, having expressed the suppressed feelings, and managed to smile and assure Zada she would be all right. The rest of the afternoon was spent cuddling Edna and talking about Zada's plans, once her child was born. By the time John returned to pick Leona up, the tears had dried, and the self-assured, strong woman was back, no worse for the wear.

The next day, leaving her father brought another onslaught of tears, but they were quickly dried and the couple boarded the train. The long return trip proved to have extra challenges, and so both John and Leona were very relieved to be coming into the station after a difficult day and night with a newborn. John helped his family off the train and spotted Johnny. Again this friend proved to be a Godsend, as he ushered his charges into the wagon and delivered them safe and sound to their little cabin.

Afterword

Here we see the struggle continuing as these two characters attempt to meld cultures. Walls are thrown up as each tries to protect himself or herself from a possibly painful truth, while obviously loving one another. At Leona's insistence to visit town, John knows he must relent although fully aware of the probable consequences. He sees no way around it. As it turns out, John is buoyed by Leona's strong suggestion that the treatment in town will not break them. He wants to believe this. In fact, he needs to believe this. The alternative, for one who waited until the age of 36 to marry and now has a child on the way, would be unbearable.

The party thrown for Leona's welcome was another hopeful sign that with community, the two, along with their coming child, could survive in this often inhospitable climate. Leona feels both loved and respected by the Métis people. This is so important to a woman who has found herself with a new husband in a new country and without the benefit of friends or relatives to support her. Both Leona and John need to believe that love and community will solve the looming problems.

When in a budding relationship, the possibilities seem endless. The love we feel is ecstatic and there is the hope that no matter what needs to be faced, the two can join forces and be as one. At times the addition of children adds a new dimension to strengthen the relationship.

But with each month of pregnancy, Leona faced feeling both homesick and separate. Managing a marriage and all the complexities involved is challenging at best. For John and Leona and the myriad of stumbling blocks they were facing, we can see the crumbling of their valiant attempt to succeed. The optimist would know there remains still the hope of a happy ending to this tale.

Dream Catcher

Chapter 6

The next few months brought many changes to the household. Adapting to life with a newborn, which included sleepless nights and the resulting energy drain, along with worries over sniffles, lent a certain stress to John and Leona's relationship. There were many occasions when Leona's confusing feelings about her own mother, and the way she was raised, surfaced. In spite of this vulnerability, this new mother's stoic nature covered up the fact that she worried constantly about her own ability as a mother.

If John was aware of Leona's distress he did not let on, and, in fact, seemed to spend more and more time outside the cabin, either doing his chores or away with Johnny and some other Métis friends. The truth was that John had been pondering the experiences he had had as a child living in Montana. Here he had known the closeness of being a part of a very cohesive whole—the Métis lived within close proximity of other Métis, most of whom were related in some way. They had built a community which worked, played, and prayed together. Always, there were adults around for the children to be with and learn from. Even when the influx of white settlers changed the town, still the Métis had each other in this close-knit society.

For many years as an adult, after some of his family had broken up and moved out of the area and his mother had died, John needed to get away. He found work in various other communities adapting to life far different than the one in which he had been raised. John missed the old ways but with time accepted the inevitable changes.

When John met Leona, he had hoped that together the couple could build a new life in the Shaunavon area and be content and happy. He was aware that Leona was lonely and yet he felt powerless to find a solution in this town of increasing prejudice. In addition, he realized that as his family grew, financial conditions would require him to find odd jobs in town to supplement their income, and this would mean Leona would be alone more often. Rather than discuss all his thoughts with his wife, John grew more and more distant, a condition that troubled Leona greatly.

Over time, John and Leona had made a truce of sorts, still ignoring their underlying feelings, but playing the roles expected of them as new parents. John tried to be home more often and Leona convinced herself to be grateful for a husband and healthy little girl. John invited some of his Métis friends with children over to visit, and Leona enjoyed getting to know them. Her trips to town were purposely few, and so she was not exposed to the uncomfortable stares that having a child who carried many of John's features wrought. Unfortunately, mother and daughter looked so different.

When Edna reached about 10 months of age, Leona realized she was with child again. By her calculations the second little one would come sometime in November. Spring was just around the corner in Shaunavon and Leona knew that the real work of preparing the soil and planting the garden would need to begin. The soil needed attention, but to Leona a more important necessity was the preparation she had to do within her own mind. This could not be postponed.

In several months, Leona would be bringing another child into this environment of distance and community of distrust. "It is one thing for me to feel separate and lonely," thought Leona, "but I cannot continue to pretend that it would be acceptable for my children as well." She finally faced the fact that a discussion with John was necessary, even though a part of her dreaded a possible confrontation. Feeling fear at John's reaction and the possible consequences, Leona made a plan to broach the issue after supper that very day.

Once the couple had eaten, the dishes washed and little Edna tucked into bed, Leona asked John if he would like to join her for a cup of tea. As the couple sipped their tea, Leona's mood matched the coming of darkness outside.

"Leona I see that there is something on your mind. What is it?" asked John with some trepidation.

Somewhat taken aback by John's awareness of her thoughts, Leona began.

"John, I have felt a heaviness in my heart and know that we have allowed a distance to build between us. There are feelings that need to be discussed and neither of us finds this an easy task."

"Tell me, Leona," suggested John with more than a little apprehension.

"We are to be bringing another child into our lives in the fall, and although this truly is a blessing, I have such misgivings about raising our children here," admitted Leona as she gazed into her husband's eyes for any sign of his feelings.

John did not need to ask Leona what caused her to worry. He knew only too well the environment in Shaunavon, although he had hoped that somehow they would overcome the situation. He too, felt pleasure at hearing about a new baby, but with Leona's words, John could no longer deny the problem and the feelings arising within that nearly overwhelmed him. John was at a complete loss.

There was an uncomfortable few moments of silence in which Leona was determined to hear from her husband before she spoke another word.

Finally, John asked, "What is it you want to do, Leona?" while at the same time, thinking about the best way he could remove himself from this cabin and this conversation.

"I think it should be a question of what *we* want to do, shouldn't it?" answered Leona, trying without much success to keep the annoyance out of her voice.

Leona did have a plan but would have been very happy to consider another were John to suggest one. However, as she expected, John was silent on the matter.

"What will our children's futures be like in this town? Will they face similar school experiences as the ones your sisters suffered in Montana? I cannot bear the thought of it and I know no other answer than to move our family back to North Dakota."

John's face held a myriad of emotions and Leona wondered if she had built a permanent wall between them with her words.

"Please speak to me, John," begged Leona.

Instead, John gave way to his fear, got up from the table, grabbed his coat and hat and slipped out the door without a word or a glance at his wife. Leona did not see John that night or the next day or night. When at last John came trudging home and she spotted him out the kitchen window, what she saw took her breath away. Dirty and downtrodden, someone she did not recognize walked into the back door. As John approached Leona, she saw bloodshot, tear filled eyes and the odor of whiskey. Without eye contact, John told Leona he would do whatever she wished. Leona felt such guilt, but knew that any other solution was not to be found, and so she nodded and began heating water for her husband's bath.

John knew that he had to do this for Leona in order to save his marriage, although his heart was not in a move away from the home he had built and the life the couple had planned.

The next few months were the last Leona and John and Edna were to spend in their little cabin home. One more planting season, one more early harvest which neither of these mourning souls had enthusiasm for, one more very sad farewell with Johnny, and the couple, along with a toddler, boarded the train for North Dakota. Two trunks held the most important of their belongings.

This journey seemed especially long and tiring. Being 7 months along and trying to keep a 17-month-old happy was a challenge. John and Leona had found very few moments of pleasure in the last months, knowing their lives were about to change drastically.

Leona had been in touch with her father, who again generously sent money for the trip, and assured the couple they were welcome to move in with him for as long as it took for John to find work and other living arrangements to be made. It would be somewhat crowded with two more adults and two children in his little house, but Lewis was very happy to have Leona back in North Dakota. Leona was so grateful to this man who shared himself and his wealth so openly with his daughter and family.

The feelings surrounding the move and the necessity for it had again been suppressed. There was just too much pain involved, especially for John. When any emotions began to surface, John resorted to whiskey to dampen down what he could not face.

In a daze, as Edna began to sleep, Leona was taken back to the first train trip she and John had together as a newly married couple. So hopeful were they both. Leona remembered promising to compromise as they drew together their differing cultures. At that time Leona believed all things possible when two are in love.

Her mind, at this troubling time, furtively searched for hopeful moments the couple had shared. Leona's introduction to John and Johnny's Métis family and friends brought Leona such joy as she marveled at how accepted she had been. "If only," thought Leona, "we could recapture that experience and those feelings in the larger Shaunavon community." Unfortunately, Leona did not believe that to be a possibility.

Leona was trying to be optimistically hopeful that once the move was made, their lives would again settle down and they could concentrate on saving their marriage. This was not to be. Leona had finally settled Edna down for a nap and exhausted, she too fell into a deep sleep. When finally the two began to stir, Leona heard the train whistle and felt the beast begin to slow down. Looking out the window, she realized they had arrived at their destination and she had slept through several stops!

"John must be readying the luggage for departure," she said to herself.

That would be Leona's last thought before her world caved in. Nearly unable to breathe, Leona frantically searched for her husband. The porter thought perhaps the stop before the last was where he had seen John get off the train, while Leona and Edna slept. Leona was very afraid that she knew the truth—this time John had run away for good.

True to his word, Lewis was there to meet the Ouellette family, only to find a mother and a daughter both in tears. Grimly, after searching for answers and trying to comfort his distraught daughter to no avail, Lewis loaded her luggage into his wagon and shepherded the crying pair home.

Afterword

This section brought me great sadness to write. Of course, I knew the facts of the story from the outset, and yet as the deeply painful emotions of each character surfaced, I felt such compassion for my grandparents. It must be obvious to the reader that feelings of abandonment have been a recurring theme for a number of my ancestors through the years. In many cases, these feelings follow generations, and these unconscious beings wreak havoc on the lives of their loved ones, never fully understanding the roots of their pain. As I studied my grandmother's life, through letters and conversations with Grandma and other family members, I have reached the conclusion that Grandma's entire life was definitely colored by these feelings.

The history of the Métis people in my family can be documented by my research. A true gold mine for me was when I stumbled upon the book, We Know Who We Are, Métis Identity in a Montana Community by Martha Harroun Foster and published by the University of Oklahoma Press in 2006. According to Ms. Foster, this work took her directly to Lewistown where she held many interviews and asked endless questions of Métis still living in the area. The project was shared and supported by UCLA and included many scholars and the staff of many libraries.

When I saw the name Ouellette within the pages of this book and realized this was a factual account of my family, as well as the kinship bands connected to Grandfather, my excitement knew no bounds. It was from this book, as well as hours of genealogical research, that I came to "feel" the reality of this culture. This experience allowed me to believe in a people and want to paint the truth as I came to understand it. Not for the purpose of admonishing others, but for the sheer delight in connecting in a visceral way with my roots. Visceral it was too, when I found myself in tears over an account of rejection, prejudice, or displacement.

My inner guidance tells me that each generation has carried imprints of memories throughout the ages. These include outdated beliefs that have colored our behavior and often have led to painful life experiences. My grandfather's background involved centuries of struggle as his culture lost its way of life and was not accepted by others. Unfortunately, he believed himself to be a victim of his current experiences as well. This left John with few tools to consciously deal with life. Running away from the pain was, in his eyes, the only choice he could make. For my grandmother's part, abandonment began with her parents even though, at this time in her life, she was not consciously aware. In addition, the estranged relationship with her stepmother was another form of abandonment. All this affected the feelings and choices Grandmother made in her life.

In the process of writing this story, I sensed a movement and a calling to "feel" the truth of my characters. It is almost as if I were present in the period of time my ancestors lived. Perhaps on some level I was. There have been spaces of time when my tears could not be halted—when my heart nearly broke for what I perceived were the painful experiences of living. At other times, I felt the joy that arose with the discovery of a new love or the birth of a child. The spiritual sensation of life moving through me supports my belief in oneness. With that belief, comes a sense of my responsibility as a conscious individual to do my part toward healing.

I choose forgiveness as the overriding essence of my thinking now. Any other concept would be too painful and there has been enough pain as it is. Forgiveness for a nation new to the concept of "justice and fairness for all" not just for whites but for Indians, blacks, women, Irish, Germans, Italians, Hispanics, new to the idea that we could really be a "melting pot" where each ingredient would be just as rich in the stew as the others. Forgiveness for a husband who was doing the best he could based on patterns of belief which led him to feel he had no control to behave differently. Forgiveness for a wife whose fear for her children ran deep. Fear leads all of us to lives that are not representative of our true essence. Through forgiveness and love we can change these patterns and find peace.

I believe we are called, at this time in our spiritual evolution, as conscious individuals, to realize that we have the power to clear the debris that has affected our ancestors through the ages and to invite healing. With each person's healing efforts, the collective consciousness can be transmuted as well. As we let go of emotional blocks and the accompanying pain within us, we open up a space for healing the planet. Opening our hearts to spirit and allowing our lights to shine will change the world.

Chapter 7

Zada had been anxiously expecting the return of the Ouellette family. Leona had written her a confusing letter, but Zada had read between the lines and knew that this trip and the return to North Dakota might be fraught with difficulty. The strife between the two was apparent in Leona's words and the decision to move was one Zada hoped they had agreed upon. Consequently, when Lewis called Zada with the terrible news of John's disappearance and Leona's grief, her heart sank and she rushed over to be with her best friend.

Zada's first sight of her friend filled her with apprehension. Leona's eyes were nearly swollen shut from crying, her hair was tangled, and her dress was soiled. There were no words to comfort Leona, but the warmth of Zada's embrace said it all. Rather than quiz this broken woman, Zada took over providing whatever physical and emotional support she could. Little Edna was clearly upset because, even at only 17 months, she felt the impact of what was occurring around her.

Zada's own daughter, Clara, was just a few months younger than Edna, so her first chore was to feed and change each child and lay them down for a nap. Next, she went to Leona to suggest that she help her friend clean up and have something to eat. Leona said very little, but nodded and moved about as if in a trance. Lewis was very worried about his daughter's health, and thanked Zada over and over for being there for the family.

Once some of the physical needs had been taken care of, Zada led Leona back to her bed. The dark circles under Leona's eyes told Zada how little rest her friend had had. Fortunately, Leona's eyes grew heavy and, as Zada sat at her bedside holding her hand, the exhausted young woman drifted off. Zada tiptoed out into the kitchen to gain more information from Lewis.

"Lewis please tell me what you know about this tragic situation," requested Zada with concern.

"I don't think we will really understand the dilemma completely until Leona feels well enough to discuss it. She has been in such shock, little has been expressed," responded Lewis. "All I really know is that Leona slept on the train and when she woke up, John was nowhere to be seen. The search led by the porter and Leona was futile."

In the meantime, Zada suggested getting in touch with Martha, the midwife who had assisted both girls with the births of their first children. Any other plans would need to be made later, after talking to Leona. The household tasks called to her, and so while Leona and the children slept, washing the diapers and baby clothes were next on Zada's list.

Lewis had mentioned that he had a visitor who was currently out, but had been with him for a few days. Apparently, he was the son of an old friend of Lewis and had come to town thinking that he might eventually relocate and look for a job in York. The houseguest, whose name was Bartlett Kingsbury, had always thought of Lewis as a mentor of sorts ever since he had left his very large family at the age of 12 and set out on his own. Now 26, Bartlett had homesteaded in Alberta with his brothers for the last several years and was not sure whether that suited him at this point.

As the two were discussing Bart, they heard a knock on the door and Lewis ushered the young man into the sitting room. Zada observed a good-looking man with gentle eyes, heavy brows, and wavy hair. He was short in stature, but clearly a man who had worked as a physical laborer during his lifetime. Zada guessed him to be in his mid-twenties. Always an apt observer of character, as Zada conversed with Bart, she liked his mild, polite, and interested manner.

Lewis had filled Bart in on the recent events, and he expressed great sadness and empathy for Leona, as well as wonder that a man would abandon his child and wife in her delicate condition. Leona slept on, and eventually, the children woke up and began toddling around the house. Zada was very impressed with the attention Bart gave to the two little girls. He explained that he had come from a very large family and so, although never married and with no children of his own, Bart enjoyed their company.

At long last, Leona roused herself from her deep slumber and after washing up, came out into the sitting room to find Lewis, Zada, the two infants, and an individual who looked somewhat familiar. But given her confused state of mind, it was no wonder Leona could not place this gentleman.

"Oh Leona, you're up. Do you remember Bart Kingsbury? When you were a young girl, Bart stopped by and stayed for a while with us, out at the homestead, but I haven't seen him since," remarked Lewis.

"You do look familiar, but that was probably a few years ago. It is nice to see you again," said Leona with a vacant look on her face.

Lewis, always a thoughtful man asked, "Bart, can I treat you to a sundae down at the drugstore? I think the girls might have some catching up to do."

With that, the men removed themselves and Leona began recounting the recent painful events, and the history that led up to them. Leona confessed that she had pushed John into leaving Shaunavon and his home. She blamed herself for nearly chasing him away. Leona confided that she did not expect her husband to return. "John is a broken man, Zada. When I realized I was expecting our second child, I became so fearful of raising a family in Shaunavon, with its prejudice and unacceptance. I could not imagine our children growing up there. When I expressed this to John, his response was to leave the house for two days. When he came back, I knew he had been drinking. At that point, he told me he would do what I wished of him."

As Leona expressed her thoughts with surprising clarity, she realized more and more deeply that making John leave what he knew best and what gave him a feeling of pride, was a mistake. Not sure there would have been a more satisfactory solution, still Leona felt such guilt. Hanging her head in shame, Leona began crying again.

Zada was aware that she had to find the right words in this moment to distract Leona long enough to begin thinking about her next step and, hopefully, at the same time, see her way clear to forgive herself to some degree. "Leona, you had to do what you felt was right for your children. This is a mother's role. The decision was painful, I can see, but now that it has been made, let me help you make a plan for you and the children. You have Edna and a new baby in a few weeks to think about. You must dry your tears and begin anew." These were the words from her best friend that snapped Leona out of her doldrums.

Zada helped Leona begin making supper and just before Lewis and Bart returned, packed up her little daughter and headed for home, promising that she would return in the morning to be with Leona. Leona was so grateful to have both her father and Zada to lean on for a time until she decided what to do. During supper, Leona brought Lewis up to date on the last several months with John, again taking responsibility for driving John away. Lewis' advice was much like Zada's, and he gently told Leona he would always be there for her.

Bart said little, as he did not think it his place, but his eyes held such concern for this young woman whose life had been turned upside down. He was not impressed with what he heard about Leona's husband, John, and in fact, felt strangely protective of his good friend's daughter.

Although Leona had slept most of the day, the emotional strain had left her with little stamina and after the conversation had ended, she put Edna down for the night and retired to her room. Bart and Lewis had offered to do up the dishes, and soon the house was quiet, the chores done. No one knew what the next day would bring, but Leona felt, if not hopeful, at least in better condition to think about the future.

The next morning, Zada arrived as promised, and was happy to see that Leona was up, had fed and bathed Edna, and was playing with her on the floor.

"Nothing like being responsible for the care, protection, and happiness of your child to put all things in perspective," thought Zada affectionately.

Zada put Clara down on the floor with the two and hugged Leona, asking her how she felt.

"Well, a bit like I'd been run over by a tractor!" remarked Leona with good humor. "But there is much to think about and do, so I intend to shake off the dirt and make some plans. Thank you for calling Martha and setting up a meeting. I know I must think about this child and make sure all is well."

"You are strong and able, and with the help of those who love you, you will do just fine," declared Zada in her consistently positive manner. "Lewis said that you intended to write a letter to John, in Shaunavan, and see if he will respond."

"Yes, I feel I must reach out and see if there is anything we can do to keep our marriage intact. I also intend to write to John's cousin, Johnny, and see if he has heard from John. I have a feeling these will be futile attempts, but I have to try," responded Leona.

Zada offered to watch the children while Leona completed the letter writing and other tasks around the house. While the two women were busy, Lewis and Bart returned from their errands and each asked if there was anything that could be done to assist the two busy women.

Again, Zada was impressed with this gentleman, who so sincerely wanted to support the family at this time. "Well, Leona is completing letters to John and his cousin, at this moment, and it would be helpful if they were delivered to the post office." Bart responded that he would be happy to take care of that task. He knew he must keep his own counsel, concerning his feelings of contempt for a man who would abandon his wife. "Leona must do what she feels necessary," were the words Bart repeated to himself lest he interfere.

That afternoon, when Zada had taken her leave, and Bart, Lewis, and Leona were resting in the sitting room as Edna slept, the conversation was kept light for Leona's sake. Bart described his experience homesteading with three of his older brothers, George, Frederick, and a younger brother Carl, up in Medicine Hat, Alberta. Bart's eyes glowed when he mentioned a job he acquired, during his time in Canada, breaking horses for the Cavalry. But unfortunately, Bart and his older brother never got along, so Bart eventually became disillusioned. When he had saved enough of his own money, he decided he would find a job or another place to farm on his own for a change.

Leona listened to this man with the gentle manner, asked him questions about his farming techniques, and was able to distance herself, for a time, from her own troubles. She found that the two had a common interest in growing vegetables and herbs and, although talking about her garden in Shaunavon brought her some sadness, it was pleasant to discuss a subject she held so dear. Bart also depended in part on *The Farmer's Almanac* and was able to share some information about new methods, which Leona found interesting.

Over the next few weeks, as Leona's delivery time approached, the three adults had many discussions about Leona's future. No news came from Shaunavon and Leona began to accept her fate. Edna had lost their father, and Leona, the love of her life. But true to her stoic nature, Leona was ready to trudge on and do the best to provide a good life for her children. She was reticent to contact an attorney who could take care of the legal requirements, but Leona was resigned to completing this task. Consequently, in December of 1914, and after a series of meetings and attempts to contact John, the couple was divorced and Leona awarded sole custody of her children. Although paperwork was sent to Shaunavon, and the summons and complaint was published in the newspaper, John did not respond.

In the course of these difficult events, Leona delivered her second child on November 19. Fortunately, all went well with the delivery. Zada and Martha were by Leona's side and observed the beautiful baby girl, who Leona named Violet Marion. Leona thought about the fact that John would probably never see his sweet second daughter, but nevertheless, she vowed to make a home for her children, somehow.

Fortunately for this needy family, Bart was a presence in the household and assisted Leona and Lewis in everything from child care to shopping or cooking, especially when Lewis was off at his job, now part time, at the livery in town. Leona wondered what they would have done without Bart's selfless help. Bart began to feel very fond of Leona and her children and came to enjoy being a part of a family. These fond feelings and the difficult situation Leona found herself in led to some surprising decisions, during the course of both the birth, and then the ensuing court proceedings.

One afternoon, Zada had come to help with the new baby. After all the children were sleeping and the house was quiet, and over a cup of tea, Zada asked Leona a surprising question.

"Leona, have you any feelings for Bart?"

Leona's expression told Zada a great deal, and her answer was not unexpected. "Bart is a dear man and is becoming a friend. Beyond that, I do not feel capable of more at this time. John was, indeed, my one true love, and although I have been hurt deeply, imagining myself with another would be very difficult, if that is what you are getting at," answered Leona sincerely.

"Oh Leona, I understand completely. I just wish to share with you what I see happening. My conversations with Bart and my observations of him around you and the children, have led me to some perceptions. From your rational point of view and the situation you are in, I doubt you are aware of this," began Zada.

"What are you talking about my friend?" asked Leona, completely in the dark.

"I think Bart has feelings for you. I believe that he is the kind of man who would be willing to step up and be a father to your children and a husband to you. I suspect he will broach this issue with you and declare his feelings. I may be wrong, but I want you to be prepared, if indeed I am correct. I pray that you will give this some thought and decide whether you could imagine yourself making a life with Bart."

With Zada's words, Leona was speechless. She looked at her friend, nodded her head, and continued to drink her tea. Zada and Leona hugged, and soon Zada left for her own home. Leona had much to think about.

As it turned out, Zada's suspicions were correct. Bart declared his feelings and his plan. Leona was very glad she had been prepared with an answer for this gentle man. Leona expressed her gratefulness for Bart's willingness to step into the family. She was gratified to hear from Bart that he did not expect Leona to bury her feelings for her husband, but he seemed to be certain that eventually the two would have a good marriage. And that is what Bart proposed—that as soon as the divorce was legal, the couple would marry and move to Canada. Although he kept these thoughts to himself, Bart wanted to be far away from Leona's hometown and from the man who had hurt Leona so grievously.

Leona wanted Bart to be very certain he was willing to marry a woman whose heart still belonged to another, and she felt she must be honest with her new friend. Bart's reply confirmed what Zada had shared with Leona. Leona thought Bart to be the most generous soul she had ever met. When Leona answered yes to his proposal, Bart's eyes lit up. Plans began for this new phase in Bart, Leona, Edna and Violet's lives.

Bart began a discussion with Lewis the next day and apprised him of the couple's plans. Carefully, Bart broached the subject of Lewis' attachment to North Dakota, before bringing up the possibility of Lewis joining the family when they moved. Lewis shared that he had been lonely since his wife, Delia, had died and Leona had moved away. Aside from a brother of Delia's, William, Lewis had few close ties to the area. The prospect of losing Leona and his two sweet granddaughters was not a pleasant one. Lewis had become very attached to them during the past weeks.

"Lewis," Bart began, "of course we would need to discuss this with Leona, but what would you think of pulling up stakes and joining us in Canada?"

Although the thought had not occurred to him before, Lewis wondered if this might be the right path for a 58-year-old man with no wife, a rented home, and a part time job at the livery. But, not wanting to presume that Leona would be pleased with this plan, Lewis' noncommittal answer was, "Let's think about this and talk to Leona."

As it turned out, Leona was in favor of having her father with her and, in fact, felt a measure of security in this plan. Her father had been the most stable figure throughout Leona's life, and at this time of confusing change, she knew she could count on him.

Once the divorce papers were signed, there was a whirlwind of activities in the household. Bart was anxious to remove Leona and the children from the house and to begin their lives in Canada. Almost before Leona could catch her breath, Bart had purchased train tickets that would take them to Medicine Hat, Alberta, Canada, where Bart had farmed with his brothers, George, Frederick, and Carl. Bart's plan was to obtain a wagon and horses while visiting his brothers, pack up some of his tools and other belongings and then the couple, the children, and Grandpa Lewis would make their way north. Bart and Leona were to be married, and eventually to obtain their own land to farm. Little of the specifics did Bart share with Leona at this time. The young woman was clearly still in shock over the recent events. In fact, upon hearing the basic plan, it finally dawned on Leona that this was truly going to happen. Overwhelmed to no longer be able to think of herself as Mrs. John Ouellette, she wondered if she could actually carry through with this new living arrangement and a marriage to a near stranger.

Nevertheless, despite Leona's fears, and although not an auspicious time of the year for travel, the new family, including Lewis, was whisked away to the train station. Many tears were shed by Leona and Zada, both of whom felt hopeful and fearful at the same time. Leona made it clear to Zada just how much this friendship meant to her and how grateful she was that Zada had given her the strength to pick up the pieces of her life. With promises to write on all parts, the family boarded the train and began a long journey of about 600 miles and several days.

Once the children were settled, the two began to talk, each shyly sharing their feelings. Leona honestly expressed her gratitude to Bart for coming to her rescue and also admitted her fears that this might be much for him to take on. She knew there was reason to question her judgment in leaving with Bart, but a small child and an infant left little time or energy for Leona to dwell on her underlying feelings of apprehension. The decision had been made and Leona was resolved. Bart seemed completely certain that this was the right course of action and that his goal was to be a good husband and father. Because Lewis seemed to think so highly of Bart's character, Leona was more confident that this was the right thing to do. This newly abandoned, divorced mother, decided to take Bart at his word and try her best to be a good wife in return.

Afterword

The writing of this section was painful to me as I continued this tragic story of abandonment, yet again, for Leona. My grandmother, abandoned with two small children, no home, little money and fewer prospects, had to have felt such a loss of control. Neither her strong work ethic nor her intelligence would serve her at a time like this. In fact, it appeared that destiny had removed from her grasp all that she might have considered stability and order in her life.

But consider the father, who is there for her, as well as the loving loyalty of her friend, Zada, each willing and able to lift a portion of Leona's burden long enough for Leona's innate strength to return.

Enter the figure of Bartlett Kingsbury, seemingly a simple farmer who just happens to be visiting when Leona arrives. My belief system does not invite coincidence but would cleave to the idea that the Universe in all its wisdom conspired that these two individuals would find one another. The timing is documented through John and Leona's divorce papers, the birth certificate of my mother, Violet, and the marriage of Bart and Leona—all happening over the course of a few weeks. In addition, research showed that Lewis accompanied the family and lived with them for the next few years before his death.

How Bart and Leona actually met is up for conjecture. Family stories are vague and so my imagination and understanding of human nature had to play a large part in this unfolding. What I do remember of my step grandfather, Bart, gave me a basic personality of compassion and gentleness with which to work. He was a truly lovely man and someone I could easily see behaving much the way I have written him—a savior of sorts opening himself up to a ready-made family.

Since the early 1900's was not a time for a widow with two small children to succeed alone in the difficulties of prairie life, Leona would have been only too aware of her needs. First and foremost, Leona thought of herself as a mother, and that role and its requirements would have taken precedence over her feelings or misgivings about remarriage. Unlike current times, when many women have more options, Leona needed a solution to her situation, and whether or not it was something she wanted to do, her survival choice was obvious to her. Consequently, things needed to move quickly. Before she knew it she became Mrs. Bart Kingsbury.

In the writing of this section, I drew upon my experience. At the time when I was divorced with two young children, the panic that set in was very real. Although the time in history and the evident hardships were very different, the feelings of loss of control were definitely the same as I imagine any mother would have faced in similar circumstances. My path led me to complete my schooling, find a job, and eventually remarry. Through every step of the way, I felt the fear of failure hovering within me, but fortunately the support of family, friends, counselors, and professors helped me see the truth: I was capable of beginning anew.

I salute my brave grandmother. What a whirlwind of changes in a very short time! Family stories suggest that Grandma was indeed abandoned, while traveling on a train with John, and that Lewis had sent money to the couple so they could relocate. However, the existence, as I have stated before, of a close friend like Zada is from my own imaginings. I dearly hope there was this kind of support for Grandma. If that were not the case, then the courage to continue was even more remarkable.

Chapter 8

As the train roared along, Bart began to share his plans with Leona. Even through her fatigue, Leona appreciated how positive and enthusiastic Bart was. Leona's heart seemed to say, "The children and I are going to be alright," while her mind recited a myriad of potential problems that could come up.

The journey was long, but the many stops along the way allowed the couple to each take a child out of the train to breathe some fresh air. Since Leona had not gained her full strength after delivering Violet, and because he was delighted to do so, Lewis helped with this task. This required bundling up in this northern climate in December. Fortunately, no snow was evident, nor storms predicted, so the trip was not delayed. Leona began to realize how much attention Bart was giving to Edna and how the toddler had warmed up to him. "How grateful I am for this loving man in my children's lives." At the same time, of course, Leona grieved the fact that John was not taking the role of father to his children.

Along the way, Bart explained more fully the reason they were heading first to Medicine Hat where his brothers still homesteaded. "You see, Leona, I have tools and supplies as well as a horse and wagon to pick up. We will need these as we start our own farm." Bart described how the family could briefly rest up in Medicine Hat, and then the plan was to head about 70 miles north to Brooks, where the couple would marry.

Bart also expressed a desire to look for a homestead near Brooks, an area he admired in the past, and he shared with Leona that he had saved up money over the years so he could afford a small piece of land. Bart reminded Leona that they were both experienced gardeners, and since neither were afraid of hard work, he expected they would make a successful family farm. In addition, Bart was an able carpenter and he foresaw being hired for indoor work during the winter months to supplement their income. Bart had discussed these thoughts previously with Lewis, but knew he needed to be careful not to inundate Leona with more information that she was emotionally able to take in.

During all this conversation, Leona had few questions, but given all she had been through, it was not surprising to Bart that she seemed content to listen and nod as Bart outlined his ideas for settling with Leona, Lewis, and the children. He did ask at one point, "How does all this sound, Leona?"

"Whatever you wish," was Leona's brief reply. Leona's blank expression told Bart he would need to be very patient with this still delicate, fragile woman. What was actually going on in Leona's mind, at that moment, was such a painful memory it nearly took her breath away. Leona saw herself back in the little cabin in Shaunavon facing her husband. John was not looking at her. In that moment Leona could smell the liquor on John's breath, and she could see his scruffy appearance and bloodshot eyes. But the words he spoke prompted this memory.

"I'll do whatever you wish." Now Leona realized with painful clarity that she was saying nearly the same words to Bart and yet feeling John's emotions and sharing his heartache. "What have I done?" thought Leona with such guilt she hung her head and tears fell down her cheeks.

Leona realized that when she had fully trusted John in those first days of traveling a long distance, meeting his father and brother and then setting up their home in Shaunavon, she had felt such faith that their lives would be full and happy. Looking back in retrospect, Leona knew her fear had poisoned what the couple had been building. In truth, she barely recognized herself. "Where," she wondered, "did the practical and level-headed young woman go? How was she replaced with this weak woman so unsure of the next steps in her life?"

"What is it?" questioned Bart. "Is there anything I can do to help?" Bart was fully aware of the sadness that clung to Leona's being, and he felt helpless in that moment.

"I am sorry, Bart. Please forgive me. There have been a lot of changes, and I will need time to come to terms with it all," admitted Leona.

Bart wisely nodded, said no more, and allowed her the feelings she was experiencing.

Leona lost count of how many hours they had been on their journey. At last the train crossed the South Saskatchewan River and pulled into the station at Medicine Hat. Rarely had she felt so weary but two children demanded attention, so Bart and Lewis unloaded the belongings and then helped Leona carry the children off the train. A man with a broad grin approached them, and Bart introduced Leona and Lewis to Frederick, his brother. He looked to be close to Bart's age, as well as clearly from the same family, with the same strong brow, angular features, and wavy hair.

"Thank you for coming to meet us," Bart said in a sincere voice. The two men greeted each other with a warm embrace before loading items onto the wagon Frederick had driven to the train station. On the ride to the Kingsbury farm, Leona tended the children and only halfway listened to the friendly conversation between the brothers and her father. Nor did she take in the beauty of this river valley landscape so different from the prairie which the train had previously crossed.

Before long, Frederick pulled the wagon around behind the Kingsbury homestead. Leona spotted the barn, a short distance away from a handsome looking cabin. When the couple entered the cabin, they were greeting by another brother, Carl, whom Bart had shared was a few years younger. Again, the two brothers smiled and embraced, and the younger remarked how much he had missed Bart. This brother was taller and fairer than the other two siblings but had the same smile. Bart introduced Leona, Lewis, and the children, and the family was ushered into a bedroom where they could clean up after their long journey. Leona then mentioned to Bart that she knew Edna needed to be fed. Fortunately, she had nursed Violet recently on the train, and the baby was sleeping peacefully. Hopefully, she would remain so while the rest of the family had some sustenance.

Bart showed Leona to the kitchen. Frederick helped him pull together a simple meal of meat and bread. Edna ate hungrily, but Leona just picked at her food, as she had been unable to eat heartily for some time.

"Where is your older brother, George?" asked Leona. Bart replied that Frederick had explained that George was away on business and would possibly be gone during the duration of their stay."

In Leona's fuzzy mind, she seemed to remember that Bart and George had a tumultuous relationship and that was one of the reasons Bart decided to set out on his own. Since she could not be sure of her facts, she chose to say nothing and be grateful they had a place to stay for a while and rest from their trip.

"If my memory serves me, from Bart's point of view, perhaps it is best George is away at this time," thought Leona.

After supper Leona bathed and fed Edna and put her to bed on a little cot next to the bed that Leona would later sleep on. Bart had mentioned that he would bed down in George's room for their visit, and Lewis was happy to sleep in the spacious kitchen on a cot by the stove. Leona was relieved at this plan as she would be uncomfortable sharing a bed with Bart before the two were married.

"Soon enough this bridge must be crossed," thought Leona.

Leona enjoyed the company of the brothers, who clearly felt affection for one another and were most kind to her. Bart had explained to his brothers the circumstances that brought this ready-made family here to Medicine Hat. Leona felt grateful for their openness and understanding. She soon began to really relax. The feeling was most welcome and long in coming. Once Edna was asleep and the kitchen cleaned up, Bart gave Leona and Lewis a walking tour of the grounds, while Frederick, who loved young children, promised to listen for Edna and Violet.

"I can see that your homestead is in a beautiful valley, Bart." Leona found it difficult to make small talk, but put forth effort to be as pleasant as she could muster.

"Yes, Leona. Although I will have to say that I never really felt as if this was "my" homestead. I was young when this venture began, and part of the chasm between George and I began because I resented him taking a fatherly position with me. Now that I have matured, I understand that this was a natural turn of events because of the age difference. I am aware that I no longer hold it against him. But you are correct, this is a handsome valley. Since the railroad came through here and built a bridge over the South Saskatchewan, many settlers have understandably chosen this area."

Leona realized, at this point, that Bart was a man who examined his feelings and was able to change if he saw the value in it. "Perhaps I can learn some lessons from Bart. So far I have surely made a mess of my life. Mother had her shortcomings, but she always did label me stubborn to a fault. Perhaps she was correct," she thought,"

Bart spoke of the converging waterways of South Saskatchewan, Seven Persons Creek, and Ross Creek and the numerous native cottonwood trees providing a sought-after area for farms. He also mentioned that the discovery of natural gas, coal, and clay brought manufacturing to the area.

"Where did the name "Medicine Hat" originate?" asked Leona, again trying to be congenial and interested.

Bart was encouraged with Leona's questions and noticed she had a more focused expression, which the hopeful young man wanted to believe was a good sign. "I had heard that the name comes from a Blackfoot word, 'Soamis', which refers to a medicine hat or headdress made from eagle tail feathers and worn by a medicine man," answered Bart.

Bart continued to share information about the area, including the fact that the history of Alberta was closely tied to the fur trade and that, as the bison disappeared, cattle ranchers moved in to take their place. He mentioned that he had been born in Hemmingford, in Quebec, where his parents had settled to do their homesteading after emigrating from Ireland. He left home when he was a young person and joined up with his brothers who had begun their homestead in Medicine Hat.

As Leona listened to John, she recognized that these historical events were reminiscent of John's story concerning his family's bison hunting days, followed by attempts to homestead in Montana when the bison disappeared. Again Leona felt sadness for the subsequent effects brought on by the influx of white settlers. Did Bart's family represent the other side of the coin in respect to John's family? One culture was considered so separate and the other able to thrive within their community. These thoughts took hold in Leona's mind.

As Bart was talking, he noticed a frown and worried expression on Leona's face. Not wanting to call attention to her discomfort, he paused for a moment and observed Leona seeming to shake herself loose from her thoughts long enough to ask, "How long will we stay here?"

I am anxious to move on, and if we can get ready and I can gather the belongings I wish to have for our own homestead, we will leave tomorrow. It will take us two long days to get to Brooks where we will be married.

Leona hid the fact that she felt very disappointed not to be staying longer where some much-needed rest might be accomplished, but she nodded and excused herself to her room. She intended to rest her weary body and hopefully her mind, which was all too easily caught up in the past.

"I will see you in the morning, Bart. Thank you for everything. I am very grateful," remarked Leona with genuine feeling. She gave her father a hug and thanked him for all the help he had been with the children on the trip. This had enabled Leona and Bart an opportunity to talk and get to know each other.

Frederick had passed a message on to Bart from his older brother, George. Very generously, George had offered the large covered wagon kept in the barn as well as two horses for Bart's journey. Bart was grateful that, apparently, George had also forgiven the animosity that the brothers shared before Bart left for North Dakota. Thankfully, his brothers offered to help Bart and Lewis pack up the wagon with the items they would need. His intent was to shepherd the family early in the morning after breakfast and make it to Brooks as soon as possible. He was most anxious to marry Leona and begin their new lives together as man and wife.

Morning came early, and there was a rush to dress warmly and feed the family. The brothers put together dried meat, cheese, bread, and fruit to eat en route. Bart took Leona out to the wagon and showed her that he had made a small area with blankets and pillows, where Edna could be safely placed. He had even included Edna's favorite dolls to accompany her in the wagon. For baby Violet's comfort, Bart had fashioned a "bed" from the drawer of a dresser he was bringing along. Bart pointed out a tent that would provide a place for the family to sleep under the wagon that night since it would take more than a day to reach Brooks.

Leona could see some of the items Bart had packed. They included a mattress and bedding, kitchen needs, utensils, cooking pot, water keg, and a bag of flour and sugar, as well as numerous tools that Bart and Lewis would need to build the family a cabin or repair or remodel an already existing structure.

Before long, Bart and Leona were saying goodbye to the two devoted and industrious brothers. It was apparent that Bart held great affection for them, and Leona envisioned visits over the years. She climbed up next to Bart on the wagon and tucked blankets around the two of them, after securing baby Violet in her makeshift crib. Edna appeared content to stay in her little bed with her dolls for the time being, Grandpa Lewis by her side. Bart had mentioned a rooming house in which they could stay for a night or two after they reached Brooks and before the next leg of their journey to their own homestead, wherever that might end up. Leona felt weary just thinking about the days ahead, but pulled herself together and tried to be positive that all would be well.

Again the family was fortunate that the weather was moderate for the month of December and that the wagon provided such good protection, especially for the girls. After a few hours of travel, Bart stopped the horses so everyone could stretch and grab a bite to eat, Leona could nurse Violet, and the horses could be fed and watered. During this rest time, Leona again expressed her gratitude.

"Bart, you have made us feel safe and protected. I am so thankful you came along when you did and were willing to take on this ready-made family." As Leona spoke earnestly, Bart saw tears rolling down her lovely face. He wisely said nothing, but put his arm gently around Leona and hugged her affectionately. Innately, Bart knew to take things very slowly with Leona and allow her to grieve the loss of what she had had with John. At the same time, he was hopeful that Leona would one day feel the same love for her new husband. Bart longed for Leona to share his own strong feelings and for a bond to grow between the two of them.

The family continued on their journey to Brooks and as evening neared, stopped by a stream with trees for protection and set up camp for the night. The horses were fed and watered and given a good brushing. After that Bart made a fire with wood he had brought along and while Violet slept, happily full from her recent nursing, Leona prepared a simple meal for Bart, Edna, Lewis, and herself. The family sat around the fire and said a prayer before eating. After their meal, Leona watched as Bart took one of Edna's hands and Lewis the other. Bart asked the little one if she would like to go with them to look at the stream. In her not yet two-year-old way, Edna jabbered and off she toddled, happy to be free to explore this new world.

Alone at last, Leona closed her eyes, enjoying the heat of the fire and said a prayer that she would be able to keep her children safe and continue to appreciate this man who was taking her and the girls into his life. She asked God to forgive her for the ways in which she had chased the girls' father away and prayed that John would find contentment again.

When Bart, Lewis, and Edna returned, Leona was feeling much better having spoken at long last to God. With contentment, she smiled at Bart and picked Edna up to hug her. Bart was grateful to see Leona's lightening of mood and hoped it was a sign of healing. It was nearing dark and time to turn in. Bart put the tent up and had blankets for the family to snuggle between. Lewis placed his bedroll near the fire. Soon everyone was fast asleep. Bart and Leona knew they would have an early morning departure, in order to make their destination the next day.

At dawn, the adults began packing up and grabbed a bite to eat. Leona nursed Violet, and sleepy Edna began to awaken. Washing up in the stream and allowing Edna some running around time was followed by a snack for the toddler, who chose to sit on her mother's lap atop the wagon. Soon they were on their way. Bart was intent on traveling as far as possible on this second day so they could arrive at Brooks the next afternoon.

After two or three short stops, the wagon was brought to a halt and the family began to prepare for their second night on the road. Edna had been a trooper and saw the whole experience as an adventure. Violet, for her part, was happy as long as her tummy was full and her diaper was changed. Leona was grateful for the flexibility of the young. Leona's viewpoint was one of praying that the time would pass quickly and they would reach their destination as soon as possible. She realized that this expectation made the journey seem all the longer.

Finally, in the early afternoon of Sunday, December 20, 1914, the family rolled into the Canadian town of Brooks, Alberta. With the foresight of a man on a mission, Bart had written to the office of the Justice of the Peace, filled out the necessary paperwork, and made arrangements for the couple to be wed that very evening. Lewis would be their witness. Leona had the paperwork to prove her marriage dissolution from John, and so the legalities were taken care of. The boardinghouse in town provided a room for the family. Bart moved Leona and the children into their room and left with Lewis to take care of the wagon and the horses at the town's livery stable. Exhausted from their travels, Edna and Leona lay down on the bed while baby Violet drifted back to sleep after being nursed. When Bart returned, his little family was sound asleep. The men too were tired and so bunked down in the room next door.

After everyone had slept for an hour or so, it was time to clean up and make their way to Justice Johnson's home, where he would marry Bart and Leona. Of course, the children accompanied them and, in fact, were entertained by Mrs. Johnson as well as Grandpa Brys, a fact for which Leona was most grateful. When the time came for the Justice to proclaim the couple man and wife, Bart held Leona gently and just as gently kissed her. Again it brought to Leona's mind that Bart was a sensitive individual who seemed to recognize the boundaries that Leona felt at the time. "Oh how I pray I will be able to love this man and not hurt him," were the thoughts that crossed Leona's mind on this, her wedding day.

Bart was so relieved that he had accomplished this major feat of gathering Leona and her children to himself. He was anxious to be a loving husband and father and yet reminded himself of all they had been through. "I must be cautious with my new family," were the words he thought to himself.

Afterword

Loss, divorce, birth, marriage, and movement from one country to another—any one of these major life events would provide stress, depending upon the person and the support system available to them. In Bart, a near stranger, Leona was fortunate to have a much needed and dependable partner.

As we see Leona's confused mind begin to clear from the extreme shock, the reader begins to recognize the feelings Leona is harboring. The one trait for which Leona held some pride was her level-headed and practical thought system. As she questions her actions of the past, she not only judges the loss of these attributes, but she adds an unhealthy dose of guilt as well. Leona is ready to take all the blame for her "ruined marriage." Human nature declares that each of us, when faced with an experience that leaves us feeling devastated, places blame on another, on the situation itself, or on ourselves. None of these options are healthy, but often hindsight and our spiritual connections allow us to take another view.

Thankfully, for her own peace of mind, Leona does come to a time of prayer and asks God for forgiveness for all that she perceives as her failures. One only hopes there will come a time when Leona will be able to forgive herself and realize that there is no need for blame or guilt. As I envision my grandmother at this point in her life, I embrace her and whisper words I learned from a spiritual teacher into her ear, "Everyone's doing the best they can, considering the experiences they have survived. And if they could do better, they would."

There is a sign that Leona is becoming more self-aware as we examine her burgeoning relationship with Bart. Her expression of gratitude is heartfelt and her prayer to eventually be able to love her new partner gives evidence of Leona's willingness for change. She realized that Bart modeled the kind of flexibility in life that she hoped she could adopt when he described the feelings he once had for his older brother and had since changed. Bart was willing to see another's point of view and this, in effect, healed their relationship, even though the two never actually spoke about their feelings. George clearly felt affection for Bart and demonstrated this with his generous offer of supplies. Forgiveness is the key.

Bart's natural sense of empathy is evident when he realizes that healing must take place within Leona before any demands are made of her. Two people who have come together with extraordinary hills to climb—will they be able to serve each other and become loving partners? Only time will tell.

Bart and Pearl Kingsbury

Chapter 9

Bart and Lewis were aware that the children and Leona needed time to recuperate from both the recent travel as well as the lingering anxiety of recent events. Lewis volunteered to stay with his daughter and help with his grandchildren rather than accompany Bart on his exploration of properties in Bow City. To Leona then, the little town of Brooks proved to be a haven where she could catch her breath before the next part of her life journey.

Very early the morning after their marriage, this ambitious new husband and father was chomping at the bit to begin his search so he could arrive that evening. Perhaps this was where he would settle his family. After arriving in Bow City, Bart found the livery and the general store and announced his intention of scouting around for any property available, preferably with an already established cabin. He was introduced to a land agent and was told that adjacent to the Bow River was a prime area for settling because of access to water for the family and their eventual livestock.

Bart was directed to several properties whose land was crossed by the Bow River. One featured a somewhat run-down cabin and barn and the agent explained that the original owners had decided that farming was not for them and returned to the east. Bart investigated this first since his ready-made family would need shelter as soon as possible. Within a short time the two men had struck a deal and Bart began making plans to enlarge and improve the dwelling as well as the barn. He was encouraged because the previous owners had dug a well so water would be very convenient for the family. "I want Leona, her father and the children to be as comfortable as possible," mused this thoughtful man.

The hour was late and not wishing to travel in the dark, Bart tended to his horse and placed him in the barn and then took his bedroll and lay down in the cabin, which he had just that day purchased. Although alone, Bart felt as if he were celebrating. After all, this was the first time he actually owned a piece of land himself, although all his life he had worked hard on first his father's homestead and then his brother's. He allowed himself a moment of pride in his accomplishment. Bart was firm in the conviction that no doubts would enter his mind on this night and drifted off to sleep knowing that he would be anxious to begin his journey back to Leona early in the morning.

With first light, and feeling anxious to return to Brooks, this young man made a quick trip to the general store where he was given a hot cup of coffee and some fresh muffins made by the merchant's wife. He was then off to the livery where he purchased more oats for his horse. Before long Bart was on his way back to Brooks. His thoughts were of Leona and the children. He hoped that his new wife had regained some of her strength and was faring well while he had been away. By early evening, Bart was boarding his horse at the livery and returning to the boardinghouse. As luck would have it, the residents were enjoying a meal in the dining room and he saw his three, as well as Lewis, at the table.

Bart was encouraged to see Leona smile when she saw him, and little Edna, although clearly with a mouthful of food, jabbered at Bart and waved her little hand. Bart observed that the landlady was cradling Violet and also had a look on her face of pure contentment. "Babies seem to do that to women," thought Bart, knowing that he also was much endeared to the tiny one.

"Sit down Mr. Kingsbury," remarked Mrs. Malloy. She had developed a soft spot for Bart when she learned his people had also come originally from Ireland. "Please have something to eat."

Bart quickly washed up and then returned hungrily to the table. First kissing his wife on the cheek, Bart loaded his bowl with a generous helping of stew. The accompanying biscuits and butter were delicious! Bart felt very pleased to be finally filling his empty belly. Once Bart had had his fill, he began to share what he hoped was good fortune concerning his purchase in Bow City.

Each person at the table wished the family well and as the supper was completed, Bart led his family upstairs to their room. Once the little ones were washed, put in their bedclothes and asleep, Leona and Bart were able to speak in private about the next leg of their adventure.

"I am hopeful you will like my choice of property. The cabin needs much work but I am an able carpenter and soon will make it comfortable for you and the girls and Lewis.

Leona could see the light of excitement in Bart's eyes and although unable to share in this completely, did feel a measure of relief that the family could at last settle after what seemed a nearly unendurable string of crushing experiences. Leona could hardly believe that she had left her home in Shaunavon, lost her dear husband, birthed a child, and finally married a near stranger. Despite the whirlwind of emotions within her, Leona understood the importance of her next words.

"Bart, I am looking forward to settling in Bow City, and I trust that whatever dwelling you have chosen will suit us just fine." These words Leona was able to say with sincerity and if Bart detected a lack of joy in them, he was kind enough not to mention it. Taking each day, even each hour, as it came was Bart's true gift and it would serve the family well in coming days.

The trip took the family longer than Bart's ride had taken him and so it was quite late when they arrived in Bow City. Rather than attempt to unload the wagon at the late hour, the couple decided to sleep in the tent for one more night and face their work in the morning. Lewis chose the barn where he bedded down with the horses. They had eaten a quick meal, which had been prepared by their landlady before their journey began, and gratefully lay their heads down and slept.

Violet woke them all before the light of day, hungrily demanding her breakfast. Leona sleepily fed the child, and the hard work of the day began. Walking into the little cabin, Leona was reminded of another cabin she had entered in what seemed another life time, but, unbelievably, was but two short years before. Not allowing herself to dwell on that time, the demands of her children and a clean area in which they could be while the three adults set up the household was Leona's focus. A small rug taken from the wagon was laid in a corner and Edna was happy to play with her dolls and toys. Violet and her "drawer" were placed near her big sister.

Bart had brought fresh water from the well into the kitchen area. Leona began the tasks of sweeping and mopping. Happy to see the stove which appeared to be in working order and some shelves that had been built on the walls for storage, Leona knew that they would be able to resurrect the structure and make a cozy home for the family. Surprised at her own positive outlook, Leona was grateful for the hard work which would keep her mind from dwelling on her pain.

Bart quickly unpacked the wagon and began setting up the two bedrooms. For the time being, the children would be in Bart and Leona's room, while Lewis would sleep in the second bedroom. Eventually, the plan was to add a small room onto the house so the family would be less crowded. Bart put together the bed and placed the mattress on it, leaving the bedding to Leona's capable hands. He also added a cot for Edna. For the time being, Violet would sleep in her drawer. Bart had plans to build a crib as soon as possible.

Leona brought Violet into the bedroom and began making up the bed when she heard hammering coming from the kitchen area. Investigating the sound, she saw that Bart was putting together a table that Leona had not even been aware they had carried from Medicine Hat. She knew that four chairs had been packed in their belongings and to see that a table was part of their load was good news indeed.

As Leona began to unpack the trunks brought from Shaunavon, she was grateful that they had traveled with her family to Medicine Hat and then on the wagon to their present home. It was great comfort to have bedding, rugs, kitchen towels, curtains, and extra fabric for clothing. In addition, the quilts that Leona had made the girls as well as her own bed quilt had traveled the circuitous route. Lewis had even brought along a few linens, including the curtains Leona had handily made for his home. However, at the bottom of one of the trunks that had come from Shaunavon were some of the items made by John's mother, Angelique. It was with a heaviness in her being and tears coursing down her cheeks that, in the privacy of the bedroom, Leona lovingly returned the handmade hooked rugs and the small birch bark basket and closed the lid on, not only the trunk, but on her life with John.

There was no more time for grief, and so Leona's work continued throughout the day. Later that afternoon, she was able to light the stove and make coffee and biscuits. Together with some dried meat and canned applesauce, which had come from the brothers in Medicine Hat, a quick meal was eaten at the table in the Kingsbury's new kitchen. The cabin still looked pretty sparse, but Leona felt a new measure of security. "We will be alright," she promised herself.

Bart proved to be a very hard worker, and the next morning was up very early making a list of items he would need to buy at the farm supply in town. There were some necessary repairs to the roof and to one wall of the cabin. The barn was also in need of repair. The couple decided to pack the family up in the wagon and head to town so Leona could purchase some items at the general store, while Bart took care of the supplies he needed. Lewis stayed behind to complete some household chores.

The response of the townspeople to the newcomers was very different from that which Leona had experienced in Shaunavon. The merchants at the general store were most welcoming and expressed their pleasure at the family moving into the area. Little Edna was admired and the baby was fawned over as well. On the one hand, Leona was relieved to be accepted in this way, but a part of her still held regret and resentment that the fact that Leona had married a Métis carried such prejudice by so many.

Once home, Bart began his repairs. Leona was impressed by the skill with which Bart and Lewis improved the little house. Over the course of the next few weeks, both the barn and the house began to look well-tended. The weather was still cold, and since the garden could not yet be planted, the family lived off canned goods that Leona had prepared the summer before as well as the meat that Bart and Lewis obtained through their traps and the fish they caught in the nearby river.

Before long the weather changed. It was time for the hard work of preparing the soil and planting a garden. In addition, Bart had built a chicken pen and purchased chickens for eggs and the occasional chicken stew. A cow had also been purchased, and it was a relief to have fresh milk and butter to add to the family's nourishment. As it was on the homestead in Shaunavon, the work seemed endless, and the couple was tired out by day's end. The girls were growing and seemed to be thriving, and for that Leona felt content. Lewis was a Godsend because he so happily enjoyed his role as Grandpa.

Leona was feeling a real affection for Bart if not the passionate feeling of love she had experienced with John. Bart felt the change in his wife and was encouraged that the two were developing a growing intimacy, despite the demands of existence on the prairie. The couple worked together, were raising children together, and were becoming very close. Bart was very pleased, when in the fall of 1915, Leona shared that a child would be born that summer. Leona had watched Bart step into the role of father and show warmth and love to Edna and Violet, and so was very happy that her husband would have a natural child as well. Grandfather Brys was also pleased to be expecting a new grandchild.

The girl child was born on June 22, 1916, and was as fair as her sisters were dark. The couple chose the name Louise Estelle for this new member of the family. The girls enjoyed each other, and, close in age, became fast friends. As soon as Louise could toddle about, the older ones would take her little hands and march around the farm with the seeming intent of getting as dirty as possible. Leona spent much of her time sewing and washing their clothing and finally purchased black instead of white cotton fabric with which to make their bloomers. At least they might last two days before needing to be washed!

The Kingsbury's were happy in their little cabin on the prairie. The farm and the children kept them very busy. They each felt contentment in what they were building together. The community was very small and Leona did wish she had developed a friendship like she had had with Zada, but neighbors were few and far between. Bart had a few carpentry jobs outside the home but not as many as he had envisioned.

After five years of hard work on the prairie, the couple began discussing a move. The newspapers had described the northwest of the United States as an up and coming area, with both Seattle and Portland major cities. Seattle had a population of over 300,000 and Portland 250,000. Their little town had never amounted to much, as the promise of the railroad coming through never materialized, and everything from good schools for the girls, as well as supplies, were hard to come by. Perhaps they would end up in the northwest.

The Kingsburys counted themselves lucky when a rancher offered to purchase their land, and they readily agreed. Now they would have money to travel west and, perhaps, purchase a small house in a town with the possibilities for work. Bart had become an excellent carpenter, a skill he would truly love to expand upon. Leona held out the hope that her interest in architecture would somehow be incorporated into Bart's work. The planning had begun.

Afterword

I remember my Grandfather Bart as an industrious man unafraid of hard work and as a talented carpenter. My father was often heard complimenting the work that Grandpa did. Given this gift, it would stand to reason that Bart would have taken pride in providing a comfortable space for his new family in their first home together.

In Grandpa's later years, the daughters and granddaughters would house him and often during those visits he would repair or build items. Among other things, our family home sported an unusually fine screen door for our patio with a handsome wood frame thanks to Grandpa Bart. I loved having Grandpa visit us, but as a child I was terrified of the asthma which plagued his health as he aged. In the morning, Grandpa would wheeze and try to catch his breath and I was just sure he was dying. He could tell that I was upset for him and lovingly assured me that he was alright and this would pass after he had been up awhile. I never was completely comfortable for him and hovered, not knowing what in the world I could do but never-the-less needing to let him know I cared.

One of my favorite memories included visiting Grandpa in Marysville, Washington, where he had built a wonderful little cabin on the Tulalip Indian reservation. The cabin featured a woodstove for heating as well as cooking, a large dining room table in the main room where the family could eat or play games, and plenty of room to lay sleeping bags for overnight stays. I still remember how Grandpa taught me, at about the age of 10, how to play twenty-one, my first and only foray into gambling, albeit we were only playing for pennies. When we weren't inside we played baseball in the large, grassy field out front or we would walk down to the beach to collect rocks or shells. The kindness and patience of this kind man made him very easy to love.

When I think of my Grandmother's mostly serious and somewhat nervous nature I have great empathy for what she must have been going through back in 1914. Letting go of worries or painful experiences was an uphill battle for Grandma her entire life. In this case, being such a young woman must have made the situation even more fraught with challenge. On the other hand, given how much Grandma valued hard work, I imagine this attribute would have served her well in settling her second home at this young age. Too much time on one's hands would have meant dwelling on conditions for which she had no control, whereas rolling up her sleeves, cleaning, cooking, sewing, gardening and taking care of her children would keep Grandma's worries at bay. I loved the family story about Grandma making black bloomers for the girls because they would continually come in filthy from rolling down muddy hills. This is a clever example of Grandma's problem-solving skills!

Her tendency, however, to set aside feelings and replace them with any distraction possible can prolong emotional pain. This was a lesson that many of us have learned through experience. No doubt life on the prairie under these circumstances would have left Grandma with little time for contemplation even had she been aware of the rewards of facing and then moving through doubts and fears. We fear losing control most of all and my sense is that this stoic German woman was in the throes of just such fear. At least at this point if not totally happy, Grandma would have regained a small sense of being able to take charge of her life. But all of us know how life happens and that control so easily slips away.

Pearl and Bart Kingsbury

Chapter 10

Leona and Bart discussed their plan for immigrating to the states. Since they didn't know for sure where they would end up, they decided to begin their journey by packing up as much as they could carry in their wagon and heading for Montana as their first destination in the States. Traveling with three small children is never easy, but they felt that taking along their most prized possessions would be less uprooting for everyone. At this point in 1919, Edna was 7, Violet 6, and Louise 4. Grandpa, of course, would be with them every step of the way.

The goal on this first leg of the journey was to cross the border and reach Sweet Grass, Montana. Not wishing to be cooped up in a wagon with 3 busy little girls for extended periods, the trip took 4 days. The children fortunately thought the trip exciting and were happy as long as their tummies were full and they were allowed to run and play often. The weather was mild since they were traveling in June. Leona and Bart enjoyed watching their active girls run like the wind, play chase with one another, and giggle until their sides hurt. Both parents smiled as they realized how happy their children were.

One evening, while enjoying the children's antics, Bart ran a plan by his wife. "Leona, I am thinking I'd like to find work along our way so we don't deplete our nest egg before we reach whatever destination calls to us. What do you think?"

Leona responded truthfully, "I am sure your idea is a practical one, and although I dread being on the road longer, I have to agree with you. If you can find work, it would be good for the family finances."

"Lewis, I'm thinking I'd like to take William, your brother-in-law, up on his offer to help me get work with the railroad," suggested Bart. A telegram was sent to William and Bart, before long, began doing railroad maintenance work. The work was hard labor, but Bart was young and strong. Consequently, the family moved often from Montana to Idaho and eventually to Washington. Everyone became tired of traveling and not really having a home.

Living out of their wagon part of the time, renting small cabins, or just setting up their tent, Leona longed for a more permanent home. Having the children underfoot in a small area tried Leona's nerves. She found herself scolding them often. The girls soon discovered that keeping out of Mama's way during one of her "moods" was a good bet. The decision that they had enough of traveling in this manner was a relief, even though the couple found it necessary to sell many of their belongings so they could travel by train. News of the beautiful country in Washington led them to Lyman, Washington, in 1922, where Leona and Bart were hopeful they could set down some roots.

Leona's first view of northwestern Washington, which sported the beautiful Skagit River Valley lined with majestic evergreen trees, made her feel as if she had come home. She couldn't really explain it, but there was something about the smell of this area that made her smile. "Oh Bart, this is such beautiful country. I hope we can make a home here!" exclaimed Leona.

Bart was thrilled to see Leona so happy and was determined that he would do his best to provide a home here for his wife. He knew he could find work at the Skagit Mill if he decided to leave his railroad job. Working close to home would enable the family to stay in one place for a time. The couple were happy to find that the little town employed a teacher and the school building sat on a beautiful site near the riverbank. The girls were all school age and their parents felt they needed some routine in their vagabond lives. Edna was 9, Violet 8, and Louise 6. Leona soon learned from the neighbors that the Skagit Indians of the area were peaceable and congenial and that many transported their children across the river to go to the school the girls would be attending. Leona felt no prejudice among the settlers against the Indians and was hopeful that her children would have Indian playmates.

Often she thought of John, wished him well, and prayed that he would find happiness again. All Leona had to do was look into the beautiful brown eyes of her two oldest children to think of John. Despite the painful experiences she had had, Leona felt blessed that she had two children who could remind her of her first love.

The little family enjoyed a year of "settling" but May 10, 1923 was a very sad day for them all. Grandpa Brys died at the age of 67 after a long illness. The girls were devastated because this man had been with them for their entire lives. Edna had been an infant but had no memories that did not include her grandfather. Leona had felt very close to her father and so also felt the loss intensely. Bart had known Lewis for a number of years and particularly the last 8 years had brought them even closer, working together to make a home for the family. Lewis would be missed.

"Now," Bart thought to himself," I have a task that I dread but I will be man enough to face it!" In addition to the pain upon losing a close friend, Bart was struggling with the knowledge that he could no longer carry a burden that had made him feel guilty for years. He had a secret that he felt such fear about disclosing on the one hand, and on the other, a very clear voice within him urged him to be truthful. Several weeks after the family had buried their loved one, and Bart felt some healing had taken place in his little family, he asked Leona to sit with him in the cheery little kitchen area which Leona had made bright and inviting with the checkered curtains and matching tablecloth.

"Leona, I have something to share with you that may be very difficult for you to hear. I would not hurt you for the world but I have to confess that I have been keeping it from you. When you and I met and decided to marry, William shared with me something that he made me promise I would not divulge until Lewis had passed away. I was always uncomfortable with this deceit but William encouraged me to protect Lewis. I am very much afraid you may not appreciate my complicity in this."

By this time, Leona was squirming in her seat and feeling scared and frustrated with Bart's words. "Please, Bart, just spit it out!"

"Yes, yes. I am sorry," replied Bart.

"Lewis and Delia are not your birth parents," declared Bart finally.

The dazed expression in Leona's eyes spoke volumes. "What in the world are you talking about?" demanded Leona.

"When you were 8 months old, your birth mother, Mary Mattman, died. Your father, Henry Mattman, left you with his sister because he had to go to the forest for work. She in turn gave you to Lewis and Delia. This occurred in Duluth, Minnesota. The Brys's left Minnesota and settled in North Dakota where you were raised."

Leona stared solemnly at Bart who noticed his wife's whole body shaking. "Leona, please say something," begged Bart who was beginning to worry.

In truth, Leona had so many questions whirling around in her head, she didn't know which one to ask first. She felt her heart pounding and realized her hands were sweating as well. Taking several deep breaths, Leona's natural curiosity took over and the questions began to pour out of her.

"Where is Henry Mattman now? Why was this a secret? Was I stolen or did my father give me up? Was Leona my given name?"

The questions poured out of Leona almost as if they had been held in check for her entire life.

"Leona, I suspect I only know part of the story. At the time that William begged me to keep the secret because it would upset Lewis so much, I wondered if I should demand more answers and if I should tell you. I worried so about your state of mind as it was during that period of time. You had been through so much, had just given birth to a child and were facing another move, another marriage. I wasn't sure how much more you could take. Then, as the years wore on and Lewis was such a beloved father and grandpa, I just couldn't broach the subject. I knew, however, that once we lost Lewis, you had a right to know the truth."

"Yes, the truth," said Leona with little enthusiasm. "Bart, I believe I will have a lie down. Please deal with the children when they come home from playing with their friends."

The family rules were that the older girls were expected to take care of their sister, now 7, tidy the house, and stay within sight of their home.

Leona was a strict mother and would brook no arguments from her daughters. In truth, they were a little afraid of her and would always look forward to their father's return from work. Their father seldom raised his voice and seemed to take delight in whatever the girls did. Lately though, the girls were confused. Their mother was often in her bedroom asking not to be disturbed or she would fly off the handle when there was too much noise. This unhappy household led to an unfortunate side effect when Edna began wetting the bed. In order not to raise their mother's ire, the sheets would be quickly removed and the girls would wash and dry them while their mother slept or was away from the house. Their father seemed much less joyful as well and his return from work was not as happy an occasion.

When Bart had shared the secret with Leona, her reaction was unexpected. Bart was sure that he would rather have had Leona fly into a rage than to behave in such a controlled, stiff, unemotional manner. He knew his wife was rarely predictable, but Bart was becoming concerned that she was experiencing a state of shock. He decided he needed to give her time and so his course of action was to maintain the household as best he could. In an effort to help Leona solve their problem, Bart remembered how intrigued he had always been by the ads in magazines and newspapers looking for missing people. His soft heart would imagine that the persons would be united thanks to the efforts made. This time he felt some dissonance. He had known the Brys' for many years and was almost afraid to know the truth—Did Lewis and Delia steal Leona? Why was this such a secret and why did they change her name?

Bart promised himself he would do everything in his power to discover more about Leona's roots and to make a plan for finding Henry Mattman. One night after supper when the girls were tucked into bed, Bart knocked on the bedroom door and asked if he could come in to talk. Leona's answer was weak but she replied that Bart could come in. Over time as Leona began to recover from the shock of Bart's news, she had begun to formulate a plan which would involve discovering what she could about these revelations.

"Are you terribly mad at me for keeping this information hidden?" asked Bart dreading Leona's answer.

"I know that I am feeling hurt and betrayed. But who should I be mad at? My mother for dying? My father for leaving? His sister for not wanting me? You for keeping this a secret? Or the Brys' for keeping this information from me, changing my name and moving me across country? I am very confused at this moment," declared Leona in a shaky voice.

"I have been making a plan to find Henry Mattman," confessed Bart. "He would be the only person at this point in time who can answer some of our questions. I have seen ads in magazines from time to time and in newspapers asking for anyone with information about the whereabouts of loved ones. I suggest we begin by putting ads in some of these publications. We should also look for ads placed by a father, searching for a daughter who would have been born the 18th of September, 1893. Hopefully, the Brys' did not lie to you about your birthday. Did you ever see a birth certificate?"

"No, as a matter of fact, I asked Mother about that and she said it had been lost. I imagine that was a lie too."

Bart and Leona decided to say nothing to the girls until, and if, their search turned up anything. After all, Grandpa Brys was the only grandpa they had known and they had loved him dearly. The couple began by putting ads in the magazines they had recently acquired. Leona enjoyed *Collier's*, a magazine whose emphasis was on news, social reform and investigative journalism. In addition, both of the Kingsbury's enjoyed *The Saturday Evening Post* which had current event articles, human interest pieces, stories, and a letter column. *McClure's*, with its political and literary content published novels in progress which Leona enjoyed reading. To all of these, the couple sent personal ads asking for help with any information their readers might have on Henry Mattman.

Leona grew increasingly nervous and unhappy with each passing month in which there were no letters answering their requests for information. But finally, after two years of searching, a telegram arrived for Leona. The answer to her prayers had come. Henry Mattman was coming to visit the Kingsbury's! It was almost too much to hope for! Leona's critical mind began to nearly dread something she thought she had been looking forward to.

When Leona addressed her worries to Bart, he reassured her that, in his opinion, her reaction was normal. After all, facing the idea that much of her life had been a lie and that Leona may not be who she thought she was would throw anyone into turmoil. In Bart's tender, understanding way, he reached out to this woman who had been through so much and whom he loved dearly.

"I will be with you every step of the way. I only hope you can forgive me for keeping this secret from you," remarked Bart. In fact, Bart had been worrying about whether Leona would hold this against him. It was difficult to tell whether Leona's attitude of late was due to disaffection with her husband or frustration over not receiving information about her identity. Bart suspected it was a combination of the two and many other feelings that were arising out of this complex woman's being.

"Bart, I appreciate how much help you have been these many months with my dilemma. I know I have been short with you and the children and not very pleasant to be around. As far as your culpability, I am not sure I would have acted differently than you did given the remarkable set of circumstances at the time. I probably would have completely fallen apart if I'd known the truth when you and I married. Perhaps it was for the best after all. Now my focus must be on discovering how this situation occurred. My mind will not allow me to rest until I have spoken with Mr. Mattman," emphasized Leona. The wait began.

Afterword

This portion of the story of my grandmother was based on census materials which showed the emigration of the family from Alberta,

Canada, to the states, specifically Sweet Grass, Montana, on the first leg of the journey and then west to Idaho and eventually ending up in Lyman, Washington. In my research of the Lyman area in the 1920's, I learned of the peaceable Skagit Indians who attended school with the white settlers. I would like to think that Leona would be pleased, given her experience with the Métis culture and her obvious lack of prejudice toward other races. According to family stories from my Aunt Louise, at this point in time, Leona had not shared with Edna or Violet their mixed race heritage. In fact, it was not until Edna was about 16 and Violet 14 that the census records show a name change for the girls from Kingsbury to Ouellette. Despite this, Leona would more than likely feel that being a part of a successful community made up of white and Indian cultures would be a positive influence in her children's lives.

I believe that John would often be on Leona's mind. Through letters and vague comments made by my Mother, Violet, Leona never forgot her first love. In one letter written to my older sister, Jeannette, Leona spoke of getting together and talking to her about John and gifting her wedding ring to Jeannette. Unfortunately, Grandma's death came and the discussion never took place.

It is regrettable that I never discussed Grandma's background or feelings with her. Even so, I have made a case for Leona being fearful of raising her daughters in a prejudiced community and that that was a major factor in the dissolution of her marriage. That being my premise, I am also quite sure that Leona would have taken a great deal of responsibility for the failure of their marriage and carried guilt with her for many years. Don't we all wonder about our past: if only I had handled this situation or person differently, could I have prevented the misery that followed? Because I have firsthand knowledge that none of Leona's children judged others based on their race, I believe that Leona valued and taught an unbiased and fair view of others.

It is in this portion of my tale that we hear of William, Lewis' brother-in-law. Early on when Leona was young, William shows up on the census as living with the Brys' family. As my research and my cousin's research developed we found that William had been instrumental in helping Bart get a job with the railroad. Clearly, Lewis and/or Bart had been in touch with him over the years. Toward the end of this chapter, of course, we see the part William played in keeping the secret of Leona's birth from her. My grandma's story and the myriad of choices all of us must make over the course of our lives, the connections we make with others, including the judgments and fear laden advice or responses, reminds me just how much influence we have on one another be it for good or bad. As the story suggests, things are not always black and white when it comes to human dealings. We each have our own perceptions and our own truths and we act accordingly. It is difficult to make a determination as to how my grandmother looked at this new information. In one letter, she spoke to a new understanding, on her part, as to why she never felt loved by her mother. My sense is that this was not a judgment about her mother as much as an understanding at long last, "Oh, now I see what was behind the behaviors that led me to believe I was not loveable."

My suspicion is that Leona had a different relationship with her father, Lewis. I would like to think that living with the Kingsbury's for several years and developing a relationship with the children would have promoted a more loving bond than Leona ever had with her mother. In addition, research seems to point to Lewis sending money for Leona and John to travel back to North Dakota, showing his generosity with his only child.

Lewis' death and the subsequent information Leona acquired from Bart about her true birth parents would have been mind boggling for anyone. But, one who had suffered such a difficult relationship with her mother and then was abandoned by her husband must have nearly toppled whatever self-confidence Leona might have built up over the years since her divorce from John. In addition, her husband's complicity in the lie would likely further undermine Leona's faith in those around her.

I have great compassion as well, for Bart, whose job it was to release the lie and be truthful at last. Bart had to know that this could jeopardize the marriage he had built with his wife. The "facts" of this portion of the story are unknown and remain with the deceased actors in this play which one might characterize as being filled with every possible reaction: Did Leona feel deceived and angry with Bart, the Brys', Lewis and William? Was she able to forgive and find joy in finding her father? Did this secret undermine Leona's second marriage?

My decision, at least in this point in the tale, had to include Bart doing his very best to ameliorate whatever damage he may have done keeping this secret, by searching for Henry Mattman. My memory of Bart being a gentle, loving soul leads me to believe that he would have felt such dissonance being a part of a lie. Likewise, I chose to build the case for Leona forgiving him and seeing the impossible situation Bart had been put in.

These are the worthy questions each of us need to answer for ourselves on our life journeys: Is the influence I exert on others ever based on faulty judgments which lead to dishonest decisions? Am I extending fear or love in my dealings with others? Can I allow forgiveness to abide with me on a regular basis? Honest contemplation of these answers could change our lives.

The Kingsbury Girls, Violet, Louise and Edna

Chapter 11

The Kingsbury's decided to wait to share any information about Leona's birth with the children until Leona had a chance to speak at length with her birth father, Henry Mattman. On the expected day of arrival, the couple sent the girls off to school and tidied the house. Leona prepared some sandwiches to serve their guest. And then the wait began. It was excruciating because Leona already felt as if she had put her life on hold for two years before word came from Henry.

"I am so nervous, Bart," confessed Leona. Bart held his wife and assured her that he would be right beside her no matter the outcome and they would face the joy and possible sadness together.

Henry's most recent message said that he would be on the 1:00 train so by 12:30 Leona and Bart were waiting at the station. Henry described himself as a tall 52-year-old man. Leona's heart was racing and she felt nervous perspiration running down her back. Bart reminded his wife to breathe—that this was the culmination of much planning and after all, they had received word that Henry had been looking for Leona for years. That had to be a good sign that this meeting was a most welcome one for all involved.

When the train finally did arrive and the couple spotted a gentleman matching the description, the two approached the stranger. Hand in hand Leona and Bart introduced themselves to Leona's, or shall we say, Pearl's, father. Henry looked at his daughter and his words further encouraged her to remember her strength and desire to know the truth.

"My Pearl—I have been searching for you for many years and had nearly given up when I saw your advertisement. Thank goodness we are reunited. You must have as many questions as I," expressed this seemingly sincere man standing before Leona.

Leona, mulling over this new name, nodded in the affirmative, since at that moment she had not the breath to speak, took Henry's hand and led him around back of the station where a horse and buggy awaited the traveler. Bart let Henry know that their home was just a short distance away and the three climbed up into the wagon and began a visit that was unexpected and surprising.

Leona's first questions concerned her mother. Who she was? Where she had come from. Who were her people? For so many years, Leona had felt displaced in her home, mostly because of the trying relationship she had had with Delia. Now she wanted to know how that might have been different had Mary lived and she had not been separated from her father.

When the three were back at the house and settled in the kitchen with tea, sandwiches, and cookies, Leona's questions began to flow. Henry explained the circumstances that had led to meeting Mary, how they had fallen in love, and how his grandfather had attempted to stand between the young people, even to the point of injuring Henry with a whip. It was plain to see that Henry had a glass eye. It was a result of his grandfather's anger. He also explained how happy both Mary and he were in the short time they were married. They might have had little money, but their lives were full of love.

"But why did your grandfather object to my mother?" asked Leona, clearly puzzled by Henry's explanation.

"My mother and siblings lived with Grandfather after my father passed on. Grandfather was a businessman who had succeeded and was very arrogant and tended to look down on others. He considered Mary inferior since she was our housekeeper and of a lower station. If only he would have allowed himself time to get to know Mary, he would have seen what a pure and loving soul she really was. But to our great disappointment Grandfather disowned us."

During the course of Henry's words, Leona was obviously moved. Bart looked on, feeling the pain that emanated from his wife and wished there was something he could say or do to make it better. Several tears ran down her face as Henry told of their little home, how happy they were together, and how excited they both were about the birth of little Pearl. When the baby came, Henry described the sheer delight each of them took in every aspect of Pearl's development for the 8 months they were to be a family.

"Little Pearl", thought Leona. "I was a beloved and longed-for child." This was such a revelation for a woman who had experienced such abandonment in her life. Leona was struck by the possibility of what could have been.

"After my love passed on from a terrible illness, I was distraught," admitted Henry. "We buried Mary near her family home in Paynesville, Minnesota, and then you and I traveled by train back to Duluth where we had been living. Because I had no money, and none was to be forthcoming from my family, I had to find work and could not care for a child. As much as it pained me, I left you with my newly married sister. Apparently, her husband was unhappy about this arrangement and you were given to the Brys', some neighbors who expressed an interest in making a home for you."

Henry continued with this sad tale as both Bart and Leona listened with compassion for what this man had been through. During the telling of the past, Leona experienced a strange, unfamiliar sensation. Intellectually, Leona knew this story was about her, her mother, and her father. But on another level she felt so removed as if this was one of the short stories she would read in her magazines about another family.

"By the time I returned from the forest where I had accumulated enough money to make a home for you, the Brys's had left the Duluth area with no forwarding address. I scoured the neighborhood, asking questions of neighbors and friends, but to no avail. The Brys's, along with you, Pearl, had disappeared! My anger knew no bounds!"

At this point, Leona's sadness for her father snapped her back into a place of beginning to accept that this actually was her own story. Henry continued by explaining, "I was a young man whose life had been pulled out from under him and it took a long time to imagine that happiness would ever be in my future. Fortunately, ten or so years later, I met another woman, married her, and have several children. But please know that I never forgot you or your mother, in spite of all the time that has passed."

As Henry spoke, Leona saw a man who had truly mourned his loss. Compassion welled up within Leona, although the tale still seemed remote and having little to do with her. When this thought struck her, this confused woman wondered if she would ever be able to reconcile this story with her life.

Henry asked Leona to share what she would of her life since he had missed out on so much. Leona was reticent, to be truly honest, about the painful experiences of her childhood but eventually spoke of her mother and how fearful and puzzled she had been when Delia lashed out at her daughter. About Lewis, Henry could hear a more loving relationship and of this he was very glad. To have had two "parents" who did not value his daughter would have been hard for Henry to bear. As it was, knowing that Pearl had experienced so much unhappiness with a bad-tempered mother brought back the feelings of complete helplessness that Henry had experienced for such a long period of time after Pearl's disappearance.

The afternoon sped by and before the couple knew it, their children had come home from school. Louise, Violet and Edna, ages 8, 10 and 11, stopped in their tracks in the doorway when they saw a stranger sitting with their parents. Remembering their manners, the children waited for their parents to speak.

"Girls, we would like you to meet Mr. Mattman who has come to visit for a few days," remarked Bart in his calm manner. Bart had decided that he would leave it to Leona to give any information about Henry to their daughters. Leona's glance told him that she was in agreement with her husband's decision.

Hellos were given by each girl and Mr. Mattman shook each one's hand in turn.

"I am very glad to meet you," said this tall stranger.

The girls received a snack and Bart suggested he and his daughters walk down to the general store to buy a few items. Always excited for this adventure because it might mean a special treat, the foursome dashed out the door. Bart wished to leave Leona to talk privately with her father.

Henry had mentioned that for several years his family made their home in Portland, Oregon, and that he had been involved in construction work. As the two visited they realized how much they might have in common. Bart was very handy with any kind of building and Leona mentioned her interest in architecture and drawing of house plans. As the conversation continued, Leona began to trust this gentleman and to hope at some point she could actually think of him as her father.

Leona began to feel comfortable enough with Henry to speak of John and the hardships in this first marriage. "You must have noticed, Henry, that our two older children have brown eyes and hair, and that their complexions are darker than our blued eyed, blonde Louise." My first marriage was to a Métis man who was of mixed blood. Edna and Violet are his children and Louise is Bart's natural child. While explaining the difficult lives they led, Leona began to understand that she had let go of some of her own guilt surrounding John's leaving. Although she so missed her first husband, she had found comfort and warmth in this second marriage to Bart.

After this first visit ended, and Henry went to the nearby boarding house in town for the night, Leona again began to contemplate just how different her life might have been had her mother lived. There would have been love in this family and possibly siblings, a wish Leona had always had for herself. She imagined that her experience growing up in a large city like Duluth, instead of on the prairie, might have meant higher education for her as well. But as Leona thought of her three children and the great gift they represented to her, she was able to snap back into the present. Her imaginings turned to a realization of a lifting of a heavy burden from her heart. She had met her birth father. He had sought her out. Not completely confident that the feeling would last, she was, never-the-less, grateful.

The next day was a Saturday and since the plan was to see Henry again, Leona and Bart decided it was time to let the girls know who Henry really was, not just a friend, but their grandfather. The couple expected there to be many questions from their daughters but hopefully, between the three adults, answers would flow. In fact, Leona still had many questions in her mind and felt it only right that the children be part of this new family experience.

As the family sat around the breakfast table, Leona in her practical and somewhat abrupt manner, began: "Girls, the gentleman you met yesterday is my real father and so he is your real grandfather and my real name is Pearl."

The large brown eyes of the older girls and so reminiscent of their father's eyes when he was very serious, stared back at their mother as if she had suggested that the fairies were invading. Louise, on the other hand, because her personality was to take delight in nearly every aspect of life, smiled and declared, "Oh goodie! I'd love another grandpa and Mr. Mattman seemed very nice."

Finally, Violet organized herself enough to ask, "How could he be your father when Grandpa Brys was your father?" Leona was very aware of the affection the girls had for Lewis and that in the years he had lived with them, had grown attached. Leona guessed that they would feel very loyal to him and so she was careful to soften the facts which she had just heard the day before.

"I know it is difficult to understand and I have only recently learned about my birth parents." Leona began to tell about her mother's death and her father's need to go to work and leave Baby Pearl. In order not to besmirch the memory of their Grandfather Brys, Leona explained that the Brys' took care of Pearl after her mother died and fell in love with her. When they decided to move, Henry was not back from the forest where he was working so they took the baby with them to North Dakota. Henry came back and couldn't find Pearl and he had been searching for years.

"But why would they not leave an address where Mr. Mattman could find you?" asked Edna.

"No one has the answer to that question, Edna. A secret was kept for many years and now we just have to move on and be glad that at last I know who I am." As Leona related this to her daughter she was not sure she could actually move on as easily as she was asking the rest of the family to accept the new revelations.

When Henry arrived for lunch, the girls spent a good deal of time staring at this tall man with the funny eye. Eventually however, with the help of some little gifts Henry had thoughtfully brought his grandchildren, they began to warm to this new addition to their lives. By the time afternoon had rolled around, tales of their lives on the Canadian prairie and in their present little town were shared with "Grandpa."

Leona quizzed her father about his heritage and now hers as well, and found that both he and her mother, Mary, were from German stock. "All this time, the Brys' have told me my descendants were from Ireland," thought Leona. It was difficult not to feel resentment about being lied to over and over again. Not wanting any of these feelings to flow over onto her children, Leona kept reminding herself that although Henry was 52 years old and he had missed most of her life, at least they would all have a relationship with him now.

After the girls had warmed to their new grandfather, they happily went out to play with some of their friends, and the adults were left to continue with the reunion. Henry asked if the couple had ever thought about moving to a larger town such as Portland, particularly after he heard that Bart was a talented builder and Leona had dabbled in blue print drawing. He explained that the possibilities for work would be many and that the schools were very progressive.

The couple responded that their dream was to eventually relocate to either Seattle or Portland. Leona began to believe that now they had a very good reason to make the move to Portland. She could conceivably make up for the "lost" years by developing a relationship with her father. Bart had his own thoughts about the idea that had to do with more opportunities for work success and perhaps a home with space for the family. The three adults continued to discuss the advantages to a move. No decision was made, but the couple promised Henry they would give the idea serious consideration.

Before long it was time to take Henry to the train. The girls were called in to say goodbye to their "Grandpa Henry". Violet and Louise had lost their shyness and happily hugged this new family member while Edna hung back as was her way. Bart left Leona to the task of delivering Henry to the train station so she could have a few more minutes alone with her father.

On the way to the train, Henry again expressed his happiness at finding Leona. This gave her courage to speak her mind.

"Henry, I would love to get to know you as a father and I am realizing I now have half brothers and sisters. Being an only child felt very lonely at times. Perhaps I could even develop a relationship with my siblings," suggested Leona hopefully.

Henry looked lovingly at Leona for a few seconds and then looked away. He did not answer her question directly and Leona wondered at his reaction. Deciding that perhaps Henry felt as overwhelmed as she did with all they had spoken of during their visit. The topic was dropped. Once father and daughter were at the train station, the former stiff greetings of their first meeting were replaced with tender and affectionate hugs and a promise from Henry to visit again.

On the way home Leona pondered her life. Formerly believing that Leona herself was in some way at fault for Delia's often bizarre behavior, she began to accept another possibility. As a woman, Delia must have grieved the thought that she had no children of her own. Perhaps Delia felt that raising Leona would be an opportunity to have a family. Unfortunately for Leona, there just did not seem to be enough love to go around. And although Lewis was also complicit in the lie, he was clearly able to show Leona love. For this Leona felt very grateful.

Leona's feeling of gratitude multiplied as well when she realized how much she had learned about her birth parents. The story of her mother Mary's meeting with Henry began as a fairy tale which unfortunately took a sad turn. How Leona wished she could feel her mother's arms around her or remember any little aspect of being a beloved baby. Being assured that Mary had been so happy and had loved her child gave Leona a feeling of warmth, as if an empty place in her heart was filling up with light.

Out loud, Leona declared: "As of this moment I embrace the name Pearl, my father Henry, and the story of my mother's love."

Afterword

As Leona awaited the day when she would meet her father, it was easy for me to relate to the nervous anticipation she might have experienced. We all have a "story" in our minds about our family: where we grew up, how we were treated, what made us happy or sad. We have memories that are associated with those experiences and often feel joy or some measure of grief at how things turned out or how things "might have been" had we chosen differently or been born in other circumstances.

Although Leona was unhappy with much of her "story", it was something that belonged to her and presumably colored the way she thought about life. To find out that her story was less than the truth, and then to imagine a different scenario where Henry was her father and a man who loved his child enough to never give up searching for her, must have caused a great deal of dissonance in this young woman.

On the one hand, perhaps Leona had been given a gift, and as she unwrapped the layers of paper she might find her heart opening to treasure after treasure that would build a new story in her mind. On the other hand, did abandonment and loss permeate Leona's mind to such an extent that embracing a new story would be impossible? Would Leona feel that she did not deserve this happiness that was peeking at the corners of her life and be afraid to embrace it? Would she even feel deserving of being named "Pearl".

In attempting to imagine Henry's feelings I must base this on the few things I knew about this man who was my great grandfather. He loved his wife, my great grandmother, Mary, enough to give up an inheritance. He suffered for his love when he lost his eye to his angry grandfather and then suffered again when Mary left him, a widower, with an infant.

A letter written by my grandmother described what Henry explained about the day he had buried his wife and was on a train with Baby Pearl. Apparently, the baby was inconsolable, and some other women passengers on the train helped settle Pearl down. Years later, after Pearl learned the truth of her parentage and her children were adults, she visited a counselor. Pearl related the counselor's words: "You did not understand at 8 months where your mother was nor why those aspects of your life that made you feel safe and loved were suddenly gone."

Will Pearl now look at life with the idea that the cup is half empty or half full? Changing one's name, or rather claiming one's birth name, might be a meaningful expression of identity. For this woman who had suffered at the hand of a confused and obviously unhappy mother figure and whose husband of the heart had abandoned her, this may be a very difficult task.

It must have been very meaningful to Pearl to discover that her father had been searching for her. The story of her father's love for Mary and their marriage, despite Grandfather Weins' behavior, would help Pearl see that love accompanied her entry into the world. Pearl would always have that. Hopefully this knowledge would help to balance the suffering that Pearl endured.

When I visualize my grandmother driving the wagon back from the train after she dropped off her father, I see an opening in Pearl's heart where love has begun to heal. I feel the sun as it shone on Grandma's head and the breeze as it gently kissed her face. Her heart and mine are one. Her hope and her gratitude are mine.

I embrace this spirit and together we release the pain of a life spent reaching and never quite obtaining love and we know the truth: This moment in time is all there is and it is Love.

Chapter 12

After Henry's visit, life began to get back to a more normal routine. It seemed that the last year had represented such turmoil—discovering that Leona's identity was other than she believed it to be, then devoting herself to finding her father, and finally after many months, meeting Henry. All of this took a toll on family life.

Pearl's goal was to relax in the routine of life before any decisions were made about moving and to get used to her new name as well. When an opportunity arose for her to supplement the family's income with a house cleaning job for a neighbor, she welcomed the idea, thinking, "I really need this distraction and I can earn money as well."

The girls were not as excited about the prospect of their mother working. Pearl made it abundantly clear that each one would be expected to increase the chores they had already taken on. On the other hand, the older girls had felt relieved for some time that the tension and unhappiness in the household had lessened since Grandpa Henry had come to visit. Even at the young ages of 10 and 11, Violet and Edna had a sense that their mother's frame of mind had improved and they were willing to do whatever they could to maintain peace in the family.

With that in mind, after school the girls completed the household tasks, which included starting dinner and setting the table. Little Louise swept the floor and shook the rugs, while the older girls began their homework. By the time Bart returned home from his job at the mill, and Pearl from her housecleaning job, the little cabin was warm and inviting.

"Girls, we are very proud of the way you have stepped up to help the family," declared Pearl with a smile.

Edna and Violet were taken aback by this high praise, while Louise easily danced around the room, opening her arms to this lovely version of her mother. Bart, too, was impressed to see that his wife seemed genuinely happy.

Pearl now truly thought of Henry as her father and so constantly on her mind was the prospect of moving to be closer to him and his family. Pearl intended to further investigate this thought, to discuss it more with Bart, and to speak to her father again about a possible move. Pearl's organized and prudent mind needed to be assured that relocating would make sense, given that the girls were happy in their school and Bart was doing well at the mill.

Bart suggested that the family take their time, save money, and at the same time, look into job and housing possibilities, as well as schools, in Portland. "Neither you nor I have ever lived in a community as large as Portland. Remember that Henry said the population was more than 250,000 people!" declared Bart. "And Pearl, as anxious as I know you are to be close to your father, we really have no choice but to save enough money for a big move like this."

"I understand, Bart. Henry also mentioned street cars and automobiles that outnumber any you or I have seen and bridges to accommodate the traffic. All of this is a bit overwhelming to me too. But think what we have already lived through, some good news and some very bad, and you have always told me not to fear the unknown. From the time we first met, you instilled in me an attitude of not looking backward at situations that cannot be changed but to look forward with optimism. As you know, that has been very difficult for me but in this instance, I wonder, should we take Henry's word that there are opportunities for us?"

Bart was impressed with Pearl's words and could see that finding Henry had opened Pearl up to new ideas. He vowed not to stand in his wife's way. If she determined that a move must happen, he would support her and they would move as soon as their finances allowed. When Bart expressed just this sentiment Pearl smiled and said, "We'll see, Bart. We'll see."

In the meantime, Pearl seemed content to write her father and plan visits every few months. Not impulsive by nature, Pearl wondered if this was a trait she had inherited from her parents. How much was she like Henry? Pearl had questions, but knew that eventually she would be able to discover the answers. For the first time in her life, Pearl felt content, as if the weight of circumstance was no longer pulling her down.

The couple continued working and saving as much money as possible and revisited the idea of moving to Portland. During this time, Henry had indeed visited the family and the ties were strengthened between father and daughter, although Pearl wondered why she had yet to meet her father's wife and family. In fact, Henry rarely talked about them with Pearl.

But, as life has a way of throwing curve balls into the best laid plans, they were abruptly put on the back burner when Violet, who was now 12, and Louise, who was 10, came down with a serious illness. At first, the high fever was alarming and the girls were put in cool bathwater to lower their temperatures. For days, the girls complained of sore throats, headaches, and pain in the neck and back. Louise had intermittent bouts of vomiting as well. Within a week, Violet began feeling better and the parents breathed a sigh of relief that this bad case of "flu" was coming to an end. Unfortunately, their relief was short-lived when Louise's symptoms continued. She complained of severe aches on her whole left side. Pearl felt that something was very wrong and asked Bart to contact the local doctor.

The news the doctor brought, after examining Louise, struck fear into the hearts of both parents. He described it as infantile paralysis or polio. Pearl, who closely followed the country's politics, remembered reading about President Roosevelt who had been struck down with this illness before his term of office began. Now he was in a wheelchair and Pearl was frantic with worry that this would be Louise's fate as well. The doctor had little to offer the family, other than suggestions of a splint or brace to apply to Louise's affected leg.

As the days went by, severe muscle spasms in Louise's left leg caused her to spend more time in bed. It was excruciating for the family to see this once active girl confined so much of the time. Eventually, the doctor put a brace on her little leg to help her walk, although it was an awkward and heavy appliance for a little girl. No longer able to run and play with her sisters, this normally energetic girl lost some of her sparkle. Her older sisters would take turns carrying her from place to place so that she could join the fun. Baths of warm water seemed to temporarily help the muscle aches, but it was apparent that Louise was losing more and more mobility in her left side.

Bart began to feel so completely useless watching his youngest in such discomfort and he could no longer sit idly by. "Pearl," he said, "We have to do something. I think it is time to relocate and see if there is medical help for us in Portland. I have read about hospitals that have rehabilitation centers for children struck with polio. If there is anything humanly possible we can do for Louise, we must do it!" was Bart's impassioned plea.

"I agree," responded Pearl. "Our doctor in this little town has done all he can. Let's make a plan as quickly as possible."

Pearl and Bart decided to ask Henry to find them a small house to rent near him. In this way, their hope was that Henry could assist them with the transition to a new city. Through letters, Henry was aware of the extent of the illness the girls had had and the serious condition of Louise. He promised to look into treatment centers for her. Pearl had asked about Catholic schools in the area. Her Catholic faith had faded to the background after her divorce and remarriage but she wanted to consider a Catholic school for her daughters. Henry's response was encouraging. He wrote that he had found a rental for the family and that near it was the Holy Redeemer Catholic School, which he had received recommendations for from some of his acquaintances.

The family began to pack their belongings and ship household goods and furniture along ahead. Their hope was that the move would entail as few disruptions as possible. At long last, the adults shepherded their girls onto a train heading for Portland, Oregon.

Afterword

In planning a timeline for this portion of the story, I relied on the obituary date for the death of Lewis Brys, (1923) and the family story concerning Pearl and Henry's reunion which was in 1924. The first evidence of the family being in Portland, according to census reports and city directories, was 1929 although it is possible it was earlier than that by a year or two.

I like to believe that finding her father was a high point in Pearl's life and a possible respite from the high-strung being Grandma seemed to be. Grandma described that upon hearing who she really was, she came to an understanding of why her mother (Delia Brys) didn't love her. Family history tells that when Henry found Pearl he had an attorney write to Minnie, executer and sister of Mary Schwarz, Pearl's birth mother. Henry wanted his daughter to have a claim. Whether this was a successful endeavor or not, if Pearl was aware of her father's efforts, this had to have warmed her heart.

I am so grateful that the time did come when Pearl was reunited with Henry. Hopefully, he was a man able to introduce Pearl to Mary in a way that let this young woman feel a measure of peace with the knowledge that she had been an expression of love between these two individuals.

I was aware that my aunt Louise had contracted polio as a child, as had my mother, Violet. Family members were unsure of Louise's age at the time. Violet was very fortunate, having no lasting effects from the virus. My memories of Aunt Louise from the time I was a child until her death in 2008 were of a woman moving very slowly with cumbersome shoes, a left hand that was impacted by partial paralysis and later, confinement in a wheelchair.

My research into the disease itself included reports as to the lack of knowledge at that time needed to treat individuals who had contracted polio as well as a first-hand report written by Jean Harley in her book, *Go*

Beyond. Coping with Disability. This was a confusing and often deadly disease. When a limb was paralyzed in childhood as a result of polio, the muscles wasted away and the limb did not continue to develop at the same rate as the unaffected side. Doctors sometimes did surgery on feet and legs to straighten contracted muscles or correct deformities. These were, unfortunately, not always successful. According to Ms. Harley the heavy steel and leather braces led to awkward movements when walking. Often the weaker leg of an individual resulted in a drop foot, which caused falls.

My aunt was fortunate, in that her condition seemed to plateau in her teens, and she was able to set aside her braces and ugly shoes. Unable to move about with the agility of others, still Aunt Louise married and raised her children very successfully. From Ms. Hartley, I learned that later in life effects are very common in those who had suffered from childhood polio. This includes recurring muscle weakness, intense fatigue, and new joint pain. Louise, according to a daughter, was wheelchair bound by her 60's.

Family stories describe the embarrassment that Louise suffered, especially when a young teenager. She cried that she had to wear a heavy brace to school and would often take it off. At one point, Louise was taken to Seattle to the Shriner's Hospital. Doctors offered surgery on her drop foot but Pearl told Louise she was afraid she would die and so did not allow it.

I imagine what it must have been like for Pearl and Bart to be told that their daughters had contracted polio, and then to realize that their younger daughter would have paralysis on one side as a result. This must have thrown a wrench into Pearl's newfound joy at discovering her father. The calmest, most steady parent would find this an event to rock faith that life ever brings peace. Knowing what I do about Grandma's history as an abused child and the resulting nervous adult, the stories that come from family members are not surprising. These include feelings of resentment on Louise's part for not being allowed to have the surgery. From her perspective, it was more a case of her mother not wanting to stay home and miss work if the operation was allowed. One story suggested that Pearl offered Louise singing lessons instead. Perspective is everything and all I have are the viewpoints of the relatives I was fortunate enough to interview.

From one family member the description of my grandmother and the letters available describe a woman who was desirous of close relationship. From another the description was that Grandma was kind of scary and impatient, as well as not particularly nice to her husband. My personal experience is somewhere in the middle ground. Grandma was not a demonstrative individual but seemed to be happy to see us on those occasions when my mother took us calling. I loved going to see her flower gardens and to visit her numerous cats, and she clearly loved to share these parts of her life with us.

Grandma suffered from nervousness and sleeplessness during much of her life. This was expressed in her own words in letters, as well as from family members. No doubt Grandma's early life with the Brys' laid the foundation for what Grandma herself called her "neuroses."

I often wonder why I did not take the time to discuss Grandma's past with her and, more importantly, the feelings she may have carried as a result of her experiences. I believe she would have been open to revelations. I base this on inklings from letters she had written to my older sister which were very enlightening examples of her introspection in her later years. My excuses - I had a full-time job, I was raising two children - hold little weight now that she is gone. I regret skipping the short time it would have taken to be interested, to really listen and to value this woman who had lived through so much. Were that I would have had the wisdom back then to do what I now consider the reason for our being together in this life—to make connections with one another.

Again, I call on my higher Self to feel compassion for all parties involved. Life hands us situations which become problems in our eyes. I can see my aunt Louise in my mind's eye and know that I loved being around her because she was such a sweet soul with a beautiful voice! I did not identify her in the least by her disability. I am grateful to be able to view my grandmother with love and compassion as another soul, doing the best she could, loving her family with the tools she was given.

Lyman, Washiongton

Chapter 13

The trip proved to be long for the girls, particularly Louise. The older girls were able to stretch their legs and chase each other around a bit, but Louise had to be carried out of the train at the various stops. As the train approached the King Street station in Seattle, the tall buildings and many automobiles on the roads and parked at the station, struck these small-town girls who had never visited such a populated area before.

The family had time before the train took off for Portland, to go in the station and look around at the amazing building with its very impressive high ceiling. On the way, a wide-eyed Louise noticed the number of parked cars surrounding the station and asked, "Mama and Papa, can we have an automobile like one of these someday?"

Bart and Pearl smiled and replied that after they arrived in Portland, found jobs and saved some money, a car would certainly be on the top of their list. Privately, they were both thinking that owning a car would help with transporting Louise around more easily.

Louise was delighted and began remarking about the clock tower which they later discovered was 242 feet tall. The girls gawked at all the people rushing about within the station. They noticed how some of the ladies were dressed with their fine, long skirts, some with suit jackets and stylish hats. The sisters talked among themselves and agreed that no one they knew dressed in such a manner.

The adults began to see how different their lives might be in Portland and found themselves with private thoughts about how the family would transition to this seemingly new way of life. Change was not always easy for Pearl, but, considering the adjustments that she had made in the last few years, she convinced herself that she could survive and perhaps even thrive in this new environment. As far as the girls went, children seemed to adapt much better than adults to changes. Pearl was determined to make life as easy as possible, especially for Louise.

Once back on the train, the girls chattered together about all they had seen while they snacked on some treats from the picnic basket Pearl had prepared. Eventually, they drifted off to sleep and Pearl and Bart discussed their plans once Henry met them at the Portland train station and drove them to their rental home. Apparently, the house had some furniture in it. They would have to take an inventory when they arrived and see what items would need to be purchased as soon as possible. Some of their belongings had been shipped earlier and the couple were not sure whether they would have arrived or not. Henry had been so kind offering to help on these details and make arrangements to have them delivered to their new home. He promised to be there at the train station to pick them up.

"Whatever would we do without Henry and all the help he has given us?" mused Pearl. Bart agreed and remarked that they were a lucky family to have someone familiar with this big city to assist them. Privately Bart felt that Henry was trying to make up for the events that had separated him from his first child. Both of the adults were very grateful.

"I have to admit to being very excited and also apprehensive about this big step we are taking," admitted Pearl somewhat breathlessly. "I know we will be all right, but still, this seems a huge adventure!"

Bart nodded, smiled, and held his wife's hand. No words were needed. Pearl knew her husband felt sure this move was in their best interests.

As it turned out, Henry was true to his word and met the family at the station. Hugs were exchanged all around. "I can see how tiring this trip was for all of you," remarked Henry. "Let's get you to your new home!" Henry shepherded them to his truck to load it with their belongings. Everyone carried a bag and the men toted a chest between the two of them. Violet and Edna helped their little sister along. Pearl rode up front with her father and Bart and the children climbed in the back of the truck with the luggage. Henry had thoughtfully put blankets in the back for his riders' comfort. The neighborhood in northeast Portland proved to be a reasonably short distance from the train station. The family, although tired, were each trying to take in as much as they could of their surroundings. Crossing the Willamette River by bridge was an exciting adventure.

Before they knew it, Henry was pulling up to a house that was modest, but to the Kingsbury family, looked like a mansion. During the drive over, Henry was pleased to tell his daughter that he had had their shipped items delivered to the house on Tillamook Street. Pearl could hardly wait to spend the night in their new home.

The minute the girls saw the home they were to live in, they began shouting with joy. "Look at the yard and the trees and the big windows!" exclaimed Louise. Violet noticed all the close neighbors and was excited to meet new friends. Edna, who was generally the quietest of the three, ran to the front door.

Edna and Violet scampered inside after their grandfather opened the door, while Bart and Pearl helped their youngest daughter. The family spotted their old couch, end table, and comfy chair. Down the hall, the mid-sized bedroom had Violet and Edna's beds set up and next door to that, in a smaller room, stood Louise's bed. Pearl had had a discussion with her father about the bedrooms and it was agreed that it would be important for Louise to have a room next to her parents' bedroom. The light-filled kitchen with their table and chairs already set up looked onto the small backyard.

After checking out which bedrooms were theirs, Violet and Edna helped Louise and the girls went out the back door to see what else their new home held for them. Bart heard laughter and squeals when the girls discovered a tire swing on the big tree in the backyard.

"Oh Henry," remarked Pearl. "This is perfect. You have taken care of everything. How thoughtful of you. We cannot tell you how much we appreciate your efforts."

"It was my pleasure," answered Henry with a smile on his face. "I am just so glad you are here at last. I'm going to leave you to your unpacking and settling. It's obvious how tired you all are. I'll come by tomorrow and we'll talk about the schools and the information I have found about facilities that might help Louise. In the meantime, I have stocked the refrigerator and cupboards with enough to last you a while. Try to relax this first night in your new home in Portland."

The family all hugged Henry, thanked him again, and he was on his way. The girls helped Pearl unpack a large box labeled sheets and blankets, and before they knew it, made each of the beds. 'Jamas were pulled out of suitcases and put on, teeth were brushed, and three tired girls fell almost instantly to sleep.

Pearl and Bart looked at each other with relief. "We made it!" they both exclaimed together. Pearl gave Bart a hug, smiled, and pulled her husband toward their new bedroom, announcing that unpacking could wait until morning.

At that moment, Bart knew he had, at long last, been forgiven for keeping such a secret from his wife, and he was hopeful that the future would hold happiness for his entire family.

Afterword

I have imagined how different life must have been for Pearl when she and her family moved to Portland. Having spent a large part of her life on a small farm in North Dakota, rural Canada, Montana, and Washington—each of these communities much less advanced or populated than Portland, and then moving to a large and still growing city, one wonders if there were some overwhelming feelings. On the one hand, there were many more opportunities for each family member than before. On the other hand, Pearl's personality and life experiences led her to be conservative and less likely to embrace change.

Portland, at the point in time of the family's arrival, had enjoyed a large migration from rural areas. Railroads, streetcars, buses, and automobiles brought people to the city to earn a living, buy food and clothing, and enjoy the many advantages of a metropolitan area. Several bridges had been built over the Willamette and Columbia Rivers and neighborhoods had grown. This city's offerings to a family like the Kingsbury's included paved roads which led to schools and churches, medical centers, and shopping centers. The community centers and their outdoor pools were teeming with youngsters during the warm months. In addition, the now famous Rose Parade, which began in 1907, was a must see for the population. The "Rose City" sported grand floral floats and decorated vehicles.

One is assured that each of the girls was excited to discover what the city offered and that Pearl and Bart may have looked at this time in their lives with optimism.

Chapter 14

The first few days in their neighborhood was one of discovery and adventure. The older girls perused the neighborhood, met some new friends at the ball field and clearly enjoyed their new city. Not wanting their sister to feel left out, many days they stayed home and played games with Louise, or put a blanket on the grass in the backyard and read books together on the warm summer afternoons.

The family investigated transit and trolley lines, distances to shopping centers and a medical center with a doctor who might advise them about Louise's condition. One day, Pearl and the girls got on the bus, which stopped right on the corner, and did some shopping in town. Never had they seen so many items available! New shoes for school were purchased, as well as a new outfit for each of them. Afterwards, they had lunch at a drugstore counter and Pearl even treated them to sundaes! What a wonderful day!

Bart and Pearl knew they needed to find jobs, but wanted the transition to be smooth and for the girls to feel comfortable in their new city. Fortunately, some money had been saved. As it turned out, Henry, being in the building industry for many years, was instrumental in connecting Bart with carpenter's positions. Consequently, it was just a short time after their arrival that Bart found work and was hopeful that eventually, he would become a building contractor.

Before Bart's job began, Pearl wanted to make an appointment with a doctor and have Louise examined to find out if there was anything they could do for her. The older girls stayed home while Bart, Louise, and Pearl rode the bus downtown.

"Mama, I am afraid of what the doctor might do to me," admitted Louise.

"I know you have been through a lot and it has often been painful, but we have to find out if there is anything doctors can offer us so your life is easier," explained Pearl.

Louise nodded and stared thoughtfully out the bus window, dreading her visit. As it turned out, the doctor examined Louise, explained the options, and the family headed home. Pearl was extremely disappointed that there was no quick fix to the effect of the polio on Louise's left side. However, the doctor had explained that many children's lungs are affected and in order to breathe, they must spend time in a machine called an "iron lung". Both Bart and Pearl decided to be grateful this was not Louise's fate. Once Louise realized no one was going to cause her undo pain, her happy disposition returned and she entertained her parents by singing songs all the way home. Louise's naturally sunny personality and the way she dealt with life so positively, taught both her parents a lesson. Despite her disappointment, Pearl smiled at her daughter and then at Bart, appreciating this happy child.

In the fall, the girls began school at Holy Family Redeemer, which took students up to 8th grade. This would be Edna's 8th grade year, so decisions about high school would have to be made. All three girls took the city bus to and from school. This schooling was a new experience for them because their education, so far, was in a one room school house which included all ages of children. All of them enjoyed meeting friends their own age and experiencing everything from lunch at school to desks, paper, pencils, and art supplies.

Eventually, to the delight of all three sisters, Bart acquired an automobile and Louise was often transported to and from school. When the older girls had activities before or after school, they continued traveling on the bus. Edna, Violet and Louise's world was expanding. Edna would soon be moving on to high school and she approached her parents one day with her plan.

"Mother and Dad, I have been thinking," began Edna.

"Oh dear," thought Pearl. "Now what will this daughter of ours finagle us with this time?"

"I was thinking that it would make good sense if I were to enroll in Lincoln High School next year. It is ever-so-much nearer than the Catholic school," suggested Edna with an innocent look on her face.

Knowing they were being manipulated, Bart replied, "And what other reasons might there be to attend a public school?" Both parents knew full well what Edna had in mind.

Finally, the real truth came out that Edna was interested in a coed school and one with a football team. Pearl resisted this idea, but had just recently discussed with Bart the necessity of disclosing to the girls that Bart was not their birth father. Since Pearl was especially worried about Edna's reaction, she relented and told Edna she could go to Lincoln the following year. Pearl was feeling guilty to have waited so long to reveal this information.

Unfortunately, all three girls were now in the throes of teen-age hormones and tended to react in unexpected ways. One day, the parents gathered their girls in the kitchen. Pearl asked Bart to break the news, since she knew his calm manner would be preferable.

"Girls, you know that your mother and I love each of you very much. I am proud of you and cannot believe how grateful I am to have three beautiful daughters," began Bart.

At this point, the girls were looking at each other with questions in their eyes, wondering what was going on.

"We have something to share with you that we think you are mature enough to hear," continued their father. "Edna and Violet, when I married your mother, you two had already been born and your father was John Ouellette."

The questions began pouring in and Bart and Pearl answered them as best they could. Pearl explained that they did not know where John was at this time. She also explained John's origins when questions about what their father looked like were asked.

The girls each had their own thoughts on the matter. Edna responded much as had been feared. "Why would you not have told us this before now? Is there something you are ashamed of? Why would you lie to us?" Violet sat quietly mulling things over. She realized she now had an answer as to why her skin tone, dark eyes and hair were so different than her parents. Louise, who was the most sensitive of the three, cried because her sisters were only half-sisters now.

After this announcement, Edna seemed to drift further apart from the family and was rarely at home. Pearl began to rely heavily on Violet to cook and be there for Louise while Pearl was at work.

In another life event, Pearl's expectation that she would be welcomed into Henry's family did not come to pass. Finally, getting up the courage to broach the issue, Pearl just bluntly asked, "Henry, when do you think I might get to meet my half-siblings?"

Pearl's hopes were dashed when she saw the truth in Henry's eyes and declared, "You do not want to introduce me, do you?"

"No, no, no, Pearl. I would love to make you a part of my family but I made a grave mistake when I married my wife and told her nothing about Mary or you. I kept from her my search for you and so when I found you and shared the information with her, she felt betrayed. It must be apparent that I have been avoiding this issue with you," admitted Henry.

Pearl had to accept the fact that Henry's wife had no interest in any of the family developing a relationship with Pearl. She looked in the mirror, noting the tears rolling down her cheeks and asked, "Who am I? Why am I not accepted?"

The next few years proceeded with both adults working and the girls being caught up in their schooling. Although Pearl and Bart wished that their girls did not marry at such a young age, vows would be taken often. In 1931, when Violet was 17, she married, Louise at 17, married. Edna waited until she was 21 to marry.

An often unhappy and conflicted Pearl left Bart several times to return and try to make the marriage work, but, eventually, she left Portland and her husband to settle in Seattle. The story of her children and their children and their children that began in the 1800's with abandonment did not end with Pearl. The human condition of pain, suffering and guilt did not end with this family any more than did the moments of joy and peace. The duality of life continued.

Afterword

I end my story describing the abandonment that has plagued my ancestors for many years and the resulting pain from these heavy feelings. However, I choose to believe that it is possible to break these frequently destructive patterns. I see it happening in my life and in the lives of many of those around me. It may be incremental steps, but there is an "awakening" of consciousness, a stirring in those willing to make a decision to turn their attention to their own minds and behavior and what is true and real from moment to moment.

There are those individuals who "feel" this truth and are constantly in the process of retraining their minds so they can lessen the hopelessness and despair when the voice of the ego leads the way. They are beginning to accept responsibility in each moment. I have dedicated my spiritual life to being one of these "awakened" ones. It is not always easy, but to be able to say, "I have done this to myself and I must correct it. No one is to blame," is a very empowering belief and the only one that truly brings me peace.

There is no judgment of my ancestors for any of their behaviors or reactions or their reliance on their intellect. I have looked within to express my tale. And, I realize that my words are only as accurate as my perceptions of the people and events. That I have felt such compassion and love for them is based on the guidance I have received from listening to that voice within and less from my intellect. In fact, I have learned through years of asking, reading, searching and meditation that my intellect is important for my survival on this planet but my heart is what feels and trusts and allows. That Presence has led me to become so much more conscious of that voice and to know I have to surrender with humility and listen.

We humans are so caught up in creating insane perceptions of ourselves and the world around us. In Grandma's world, it was easy to see how history seemed so very unkind to her—how she could hold resentment and personal guilt for the events that occurred. Each of us holds memories of life experiences that affect us, often adversely. How we choose to remember and hold onto them can lead to blame and judgment of ourselves and others. Even more difficult are the resulting feelings and sometimes physical and mental manifestations that come from "unremembered" events. Depression, anger, and pain can direct our lives and we may be completely unaware of the source be they in the present lifetime or from our ancestors that we carry in our very genes.

Our journey takes us to a realization that we create our experience despite events we believe happened to us. Every thought, gesture, and communication we make reveals what we have allowed to percolate in our minds. What I convey tells the world what I believe about myself. We must believe the truth, at our core, that we are love. We witness the effects of the choices we have made and can begin to take responsibility for them without casting judgment and instead living in freedom. At long last we have the capacity to see that if we experience something it is because we are the source of it. We are becoming conscious enough to dissolve thoughts and perceptions that are out of alignment with what we know in our hearts is true.

As I have mentioned, I spent a good deal of time familiarizing myself and the reader with the Métis culture as I came to understand it. In the course of this study, I came across an article written to describe how the City of Vancouver was the first municipality in Canada to proclaim a "Year of Reconciliation" that began on National Aboriginal Day, June 21, 2013. There continues to be National Recognition gatherings yearly across Canada. This movement is an example of consciousness expanding across the globe. I was moved to read an elder's statement and a description of the purpose of such gatherings. In part, this is a forum for Aboriginals to speak their truths about the trauma of Indian Residential Schools and other atrocities imposed upon humans around the world. There was an acknowledgement of the pain and suffering that had been handed down from one generation to another in diverse societies. But the miracle of the meetings was the realization of the interconnectedness they had through the same mind and Spirit. They reminded each other of their traditional teachings that spoke to balance, healing, forgiveness, and unity. There was an invitation for all people to search their own traditions and beliefs and those of their ancestors with the higher purpose of discovering core values that create a peaceful, harmonious society and a healthy earth.

We all must make commitments to heal ourselves in order to affect this evolutionary raising of consciousness. We must learn that we are not separate from one another any more than a wave is separate from the ocean. The "soup" we live in is one of creative energy. We can, and are, learning to swim in this liquid gold and to transition from a painful world to one in which Love is the norm.

I am grateful to the creative energy of life that led me to express the love I feel for not only my ancestors, but for all humanity.

Bart Kingsbury, Henry (Hank) Mattman and friend

Portland, Oregon
Sept. 10, 1962

AFFIDAVIT

STATE OF OREGON)
) ss.
County of Multnomah)

    I, Pearl Ketchum of 15034 25th St. N.E., Seattle, 55, Washington, being first duly sworn, depose and say:

    That I am the mother of Louise Estelle Camp, nee Kingsbury, who was born the child of me and Bartlett Burr Kingsbury on the 22nd day of June 1916 on a farm about 10 miles south of Bow City, Alberta, Canada.

    My maiden name was Pearl Mattman, although I used the name Leona Brys at the time of marriage to Bartlett Burr Kingsbury, because I was raised by persons of that surname and was not aware that they had not adopted me, until after my said marriage.

Pearl Ketchum
Pearl Ketchum

Subscribed and sworn to before me this 10th day of Sept., 1962.

D. L. ALDERTON
Notary Public for Oregon
My Commission Expires June 23, 1966

Authentication of Pearl and Louise's Birth History

Bart Kingsbury

Bart Kingsbury & Grandchildren
at his cabin in Tulalip, Washington

Linda age 14 and Grandpa Bart at the cabin

Pearl in her 80's

Linda and Pearl

References

Books and Periodicals:
Go Beyond. Coping with Disability – Jean Hartley

The New Peoples-Being and Becoming Métis in North America – Jacqueline Peterson, Jennifer Brown editors

We Know Who We Are - Métis Identity in a Montana Community – Martha Harroun Foster

The Old Farmer's Almanac

Life On The Farm – John E. Miller

Corncob Fuel and Cold Prairie Winters – The Hometown Memories Team, August 2014

One-Room Country School – Norma C. Wilson and Charles L. Woodard

Websites:
ancestry.com
reconciliationcanada.ca
Métismuseum.ca
winnipegfreepress.com
firstpeoplesofcanada.com
Canadian Genealogy Index
whats-your-sign.com/native-american-animal-symbols
oregonpioneers.com

Census Records:
Canada, United States, State of Washington, State of Oregon

Notes